Innocent Crook

d. E. Rogers

Rogers Entertainment Group International
(REGI)

Published by Rogers Entertainment Group International

For information, please contact:

David (d. E.) Rogers at: films@derogers.com or by phone at 1-888-258-7775.

www.derogers.com

ISBN: 978-0-9708808-9-5

Printed in the United States of America

Dedication

With this being my 10th book and knowing the hard work, obstacles, and patience it takes to write just one book, I dedicate this book to the lovers of writing and reading books. Without the 2 being connected we wouldn't have such great works of art to read and talk about.

CHAPTER ONE

In the darkest and most isolated alley in Memphis, Tennessee, not far from Tom Lee Park, two cars about 20 feet apart faced each other with their headlights beaming. On the hood of one of the cars were two briefcases. One was filled with about fifty keys of cocaine and the other with over a million dollars in cash. The person looking at the cocaine was a pregnant black woman named Maggie May Jones, in her mid-twenties. She was eight and a half months pregnant. By her side were four guys holding military type weapons, watching her back closely. She and her crew were dressed like street hoodlums, torn jeans and black hoodies. The man across from them was a white male in his early forties. His name was Thomas Kennedy. He and his crew of three were dressed in business suits. He tried not to show it, but it was obvious he believed he was better than Maggie's crew by the way he stuck his nose in the air and at times spoke down to them. Though the tension was thick, all parties seemed amicable.

"Go ahead and get a taste," Thomas said staring at Maggie.

She slit her eyes at him. "You got jokes I see."

"Shouldn't you be robbing a bank or in prenatal class?" Thomas asked with a grin. "Lamaze?"

"I do what Justine needs to be done."

He looked at her stomach. "Looks like you're ready to pop any day now."

"Where's the rest of the shipment?" Maggie asked ignoring his last statement. "Mr. Kennedy, you know Justine don't like coming up short."

"That's all I have today? Let's call it a slow week," he said with a smirk.

"You think this is funny?" Maggie asked taking a step closer to him.

Thomas looked at her people and then at her. "Do you even understand the risk that I take so that you can serve your little druggies on the street? Do you? Everything you people have built is because of me."

"Am I supposed to care about old shit?" Maggie rolled her eyes at him. "You short, dawg. Where's our product?"

"Just tell your sister that next week will be better. She has my promise."

"Your promise, huh?" Maggie smiled. "Well, Justine had her own message for you."

Thomas was curious about what that message would be. "I'm listening," he said giving her his undivided attention.

"She didn't like hearing from them damn Puerto Ricans that you have been selling to them now. That's our fucking competition. You gave them our product. You didn't think they would talk. Everybody knows Puerto Ricans can't be quiet about shit." She laughed and her crew laughed. They kept a firm grip on their guns.

Thomas started to perspire a little. He swiped his brow. "Hey, they wanted to pay more than what you guys are willing to pay. It's business. I'll make sure that everybody is happy in the end," he said as his body began to tremble.

"You think we care about everybody being happy? You must be crazy. You think McDonald's is happy when Burger King's profits are up? I think you have mistaken what we do for a living. Our deal was that you would only supply to us in this city. Am I confused? Aren't we still in Memphis?"

The four guys that came with Maggie quickly drew their guns. Thomas stood there trying to figure a way out of it. Maggie stared at him shaking her head. She wished him dead based on the mere fact that he thought he was smarter than her.

"I can make this right," he said.

"Make what right? You're a selfish bastard. Our business is over with you."

Thomas cleared his throat. "But Justine needs my contact. He's the only one who can supply her demand. You want to kill the gateway for your people?"

Maggie laughed out loud. "Once again you must think we are stupid country folk. No respect from Thomas Kennedy." She laughed. "I must admit you have a cool ass name...for a headstone."

Thomas knew he needed to talk fast and slick if he had any chance of living another day. "What do you want from me?" He got on his knees to beg. "Just say it and it's done. I promise."

"Nothing. Charles Winston Jacobs is, or should I say, was your connect. After we told him that you were not supplying us with what we had agreed upon he gave you up after we cut off that left hand. Come to find out Charles hates Puerto Ricans, but loves money and a good deal. With a little persuasion, he saw things our way. Even gave us a ten percent discount."

Thomas had a blank look on his face as Maggie smiled. "You know I always hated you. Seeing people die is normally painful, but this is a celebration."

"I can make this right." Thomas had his hands extended out to her.

Maggie pulled out her gun. "Me too." She shot him in the head. His body collapsed to the ground as blood gushed from his brain. She smiled.

Thomas's people stood there waiting to get shot. Maggie's crew waited for her to give them the word. She stood there thinking for a moment on what to do.

"Only him, unless you want to die." The men shook their heads. "Well, we need some new people. You have to get better because we got the jump on you too easily. Justine likes her guys to be smarter and faster. Only speak when she gives you permission. She doesn't like cowboys."

"We will get better," one of the men said interrupting her. "I never liked that guy anyway."

With disdain, Maggie stared at the guy talking and shook her head. She then turned to walk away. "All you had to do was keep your damn mouth shut. Kill them all."

Her men shot the other men down quickly. Maggie got in the backseat of the car. "What an idiot. He should have kept his mouth shut. Didn't I say only speak when given permission? Just plain stupid!" She rubbed her plump stomach. "Man, this baby is starting to kick hard." Maggie grabbed a large notebook in the seat next to her and started to write in it.

The driver noticed. "What are you writing?"

"As always, I'm writing about life on the other side." She smiled as she looked through the moon roof at the stars. "Hopefully, I can be a good mother. I want this baby to have a better life than me. As long as I'm alive, he will be taken care of like a king."

CHAPTER TWO

---

14 Years Later

Water dripped from the ceiling slowly as the street light glimmered into the living room where Jupiter slept. The room was dark, cold, damp, and dreary. On the hard cement floor, next to him, was his six year old sister, Penelope, who everyone called Penny. Penny was a pretty, light brown skinned little girl with pigtails. She looked up to her brother to protect her against anything, and Jupiter, even at fourteen years old, did his best to do that. They had a special *'us against the world'* bond that nobody could break. Being her protector, he held her hand as they slept. Their studio apartment was on the Southside of Memphis in the Riverview neighborhood. It was small, about two hundred square feet, with dirty white walls. In it was nothing more than a couch, an air mattress, a refrigerator, and a hot plate. To them this was home. With the heat not working since last winter, it was surprising that they had survived without freezing to death. They now faced the worst winter storm on record ever for Memphis, Tennessee. Without their coats and blankets, they would definitely freeze to death.

Nearing midnight, the two children were alone and had been for hours. It was a common occurrence in their lives. Jupiter had been more than a brother to Penny; he was her father and mother as well. There wasn't anything in the world he wouldn't do or sacrifice for her.

Jupiter's eyes opened as he heard a rustling sound in the hallway outside of the front door. He moved closer to Penny and closed his eyes pretending to be asleep. Whatever or whoever it was, he knew he desperately wanted to avoid them.

The front door swung open and Maggie, now in her late thirties, stumbled in with a tall black man named Clyde. They were drunk and high on cocaine. Their eyes were bloodshot, and they smelled of the nightlife. Loud and belligerent, people in the building could hear them swearing at each other. Once inside, Maggie immediately turned on all of the lights. She went over to Jupiter and stood over him for about a minute.

"Nigga, you ain't sleep!" she said with laughter.

Jupiter kept his eyes closed and didn't move. You could see the anguish on his face while he pretended to sleep. He hoped that she would leave him alone.

Maggie kicked him in the butt. "I know you hear me. You could be sleeping on the street. Get up!" She kicked him once more. "Next time it's going to be your head."

Jupiter opened up his eyes and stared up at her. "Yes, momma," he replied.

She looked down upon him with disdain. Maggie was a bank robber and drug dealing addict. She had spent most of her life avoiding jail as a master criminal. Selling, robbing, stealing, and partying were the only skills she had. As a parent, she was probably one of the worst to live based on her non-existent parenting skills and unsupportive attitude. It didn't start out that way with Jupiter, but being a part of a crime family, she was never able to fully walk away. Maggie did try on several occasions, each time ending with her sister pressuring her to come back for the family. In her parenting history, she had tried to sell Jupiter and Penelope on several occasions, and on a regular basis she would leave them alone without anything to eat. For Maggie, her kids had become nothing more than a government check. She had no emotional ties to them nor did she want to develop any. Having lived a hard and fast life, she knew close bonds were weaknesses often exploited in her line of business. It was a common occurrence that she had witnessed many times before, where someone was destroyed because of a loved one. To leave people in the dark, Maggie told everyone, even her kids, that she didn't know who their fathers were. She felt more at ease keeping people at arm's length.

Maggie stared at him. "That's more like it! Did y'all eat?"

"No, there wasn't anything in the refrigerator," Jupiter responded sheepishly.

Maggie grew gravely concerned. "You didn't call Justine did you?"

"No, I went to Mrs. Jenkins down the hall, and she gave us something to eat."

Maggie reached down and grabbed him by his shirt. "You want me to go back to jail! I told you don't bother anybody with your mess. Don't anybody care about you eating."

Fear was all over Jupiter's face. "No momma, Penny needed to eat. I didn't tell Mrs. Jenkins anything."

Clyde, Maggie's on and off again boyfriend, looked on from behind shaking his head. Maggie caught a glimpse of his actions.

"What Clyde?" she yelled. "You think you can do a better job than me raising these kids?"

"Lower your voice now. You know Clyde don't play that," Clyde said frowning up. "These ain't Clyde's kids anyway."

Jupiter looked over and started to laugh, but quickly stopped. He knew Clyde was unstable and hated when people laughed at him for referencing himself in the third person, so he stayed quiet.

Maggie huffed. "You were shaking your head for some reason. What I do? Speak your mind."

"Can't you drop these kids off somewhere?" Clyde asked with a constipated look on his face.

Maggie twisted her neck. "These my kids, Clyde. What do you think I can do with them? Ain't nobody going take care of them but me. Maybe I should drop them off at your momma's place with your four kids that you don't see. Don't judge me!"

"They are seriously messing up my flow. I want to do some thangs to you, if you know what I mean, R rated stuff." He grabbed his crouch.

"Let's go back to your place." Maggie huffed.

"My momma and them are still up. And you know she doesn't like you."

"Who does she like?" Maggie rolled her eyes. "Do you want me or your momma?"

"Okay, I guess I'll be going. I was going to share my little bag of tricks with you." Clyde waved a plastic bag with cocaine in it at her. "I'll find somebody to appreciate Clyde."

She stared at the bag like it was a magic wand hypnotizing her. Her eyes followed every movement of the bag. "Baby, don't be like that." She started fidgeting. "Don't leave."

"Clyde's out." Clyde turned to walk out the door.

"Just for one hour," she said begging. "I got to take them to school tomorrow. Some stupid award ceremony shit. These schools always making these kids think they can be better than me."

"What you gonna do about these kids?" Clyde asked again looking directly at Jupiter.

Maggie looked around and then down at Jupiter. "Get your sister and go into the hallway." Jupiter didn't quite understand what she meant so he didn't react.

"Are you retarded? I said go to the hallway." Jupiter got up and started to head toward the door. "Fool, get your sister! I swear I'm gonna go upside your head. I don't know how your school thinks you're so smart. Dumb ass boy!"

"But she's sleeping," Jupiter replied and got slapped across the mouth. He almost fell to the floor. He held his face in his hand as he looked up at Maggie, scared of what she might do next.

"Want some more?" Maggie stared him into the ground. "Got plenty of it." She put her hand up in the air preparing to hit him again.

Jupiter quickly grabbed his sister, who was unaware of what was happening, and headed out the door. Maggie followed and slammed the door behind them. With tears in his eyes, Jupiter sat on the ground as his sister slept in his lap. Within minutes, he could hear his mother wildly having sex, at times screaming at the top of her lungs. He prayed that it would stop until he dozed off to sleep.

After an hour, things quieted down, but it would be almost five hours before he and his sister would reenter the apartment, that only happened because Clyde nearly tripped over them as he was leaving. When they came back inside, Maggie was stark naked and out cold on the air mattress. Seeing that it was near six a.m., Jupiter laid his sister on the couch and went to the shower to get ready for school. After he was dressed, he went and helped Penny get dressed. At about seven a.m., they left for school unnoticed by their drugged out mother who laid there like a dead person.

❧

That afternoon at George Washington Carver High School, the gymnasium was packed with nearly seven hundred students from the ninth grade to the 12th grade. The principal was at the podium announcing the last award for the day. The principal looked at Jupiter and then around the audience to see if he saw any of his family in attendance. Seeing no one made the principal sad, and staring into Jupiter's sorrowful eyes only made it worse. He was the only student being awarded that didn't have a parent in attendance. The seats on both sides of him were empty and only added to his isolation and seeming abandonment.

"The Mayor will be presenting our last award today. The Martin Luther King Junior Award, which is awarded every January to honor the state's best student from 9th to the 12th grade. This award goes only to the best achievers in the state. For the first time in our great city's history, a student from our school system is being recognized for his dedication and hard work. It makes me proud to say that I'm from Memphis, and that I know him. I am honored that Mayor Jacobs has come here today to honor one of our own. With no further ado, please give a warm welcome to Mayor Jacobs."

Mayor Jacobs, an older black man in his mid-fifties, stepped up to the podium. He looked around and smiled. He had been mayor for eight years and a hometown athletic hero. The people of Memphis adored him.

The mayor cleared his throat and started to speak. "I am so glad to be here today. It is always an honor to give an award to a student in our great city that has excelled in his academics and his community service to others. In my eight years as Mayor, I have never had the pleasure of bestowing this honor on any of my great citizens, but today that all changes. The student who will receive this award has been a straight A student his whole life. He has been a paperboy, great brother and son, and has volunteered countless hours feeding the homeless. This student is the apple in all his teachers eyes. He's caring, sharing, and has one of the greatest hearts around. It really makes me proud to know that students like him still exist." The mayor pointed to the students. "Take note, this young man might be mayor one day. He inspires me, just knowing that we are making a difference in our communities. Please stand up and join me in honoring our very own 2013 Martin Luther King Junior Award for Excellence winner, Jupiter Jones."

The students stood and clapped loudly for Jupiter. He slowly stood up and immediately looked around hoping to see his mother in the crowd or standing by the gym doors. He saw no one. His teacher nudged him on the shoulder to head to the stage. He slowly walked up to the podium and accepted the award. He and the mayor took pictures for the city and state newspapers.

After they finished taking pictures, the Mayor asked, "So Jupiter, where are your parents?"

Jupiter wanted to cry. He held it together pretty well. "My mother is at work. She couldn't make it."

The Mayor saw the sorrow in his eyes. "Hey, cheer up. She will have plenty more moments to share in your accomplishments. You have a very bright future, young man. You've made your city proud."

❧

Across town, in ski masks and toting high powered machine guns, Clyde and Maggie were running out of the Cadence Bank on Union Avenue, shooting their way past the guards on the way to their car outside. Once they drove off, Maggie looked down at her watch and remembered the award ceremony at Jupiter's school. Now in a high speed chase, she quickly forgot about it as she fired at the cops trying to catch them.

CHAPTER THREE

T hat same day after school, Jupiter walked over to Georgia Avenue Elementary School to pick up Penny. As he approached, he saw his sister's elated face waiting for him by the entrance. He tried to conceal the large plaque that he was awarded to avoid his sister talking about it. Being her idol, Penny loved to brag about her big brother and his accomplishments, even though she barely understood what they meant, she knew by the attention and the awards that he had received that he was very special. Jupiter walked up to her.

"How was school today?" he asked with a big smile. Jupiter loved his sister so much. She was his everything. Being her primary caregiver, outside of school they spent every minute together. It was a burden that he cherished.

Penny grabbed his hand and pulled him toward the sidewalk so they could leave the school yard.

"I had an awesome day at school," she said staring at the plaque under his arm. "What's that?" Penny smiled. "Is that your award?"

Jupiter secured it firmly under his arm as if he was hiding the award, which was impossible to do. "Nothing."

"Let me see it." Penny tried to grab it from him, but he pulled away.

"I said it's nothing," Jupiter said with sternness in his voice. He tried to hold a serious expression but couldn't. He started laughing at himself. "Okay Penny, if I show you this, you can't tell anybody about it, even mom."

"Why not mom? She'll be proud of you."

Jupiter rolled his eyes. She was the last person he thought would be proud of it. "Not even mom. She doesn't understand or care." He stopped in his tracks and turned to his little sister. He looked her in the eyes. By Penny's blank face, he could tell he had her undivided attention. "Penny, I know you love mom and I do too, but mom doesn't quite feel the same about us as we do about her. I wish things were different, but that's how she is and probably will always be. I know you're too young to understand everything that's going on, but I hope you know one thing for sure, and that is that I will never leave you or let something bad happen to you. Team one for life." He raised his hand up for his sister to give him a high-five, which she quickly did.

"Team one," she said with a grin on her face as they continued their walk toward home.

∽

About thirty minutes later, Jupiter and Penny arrived home. When they entered, about four hand guns were pointed at their heads. Jupiter placed Penny behind him to protect her. Behind the guns, he saw his mother staring at them. The annoyed look on her face was a familiar one to them. On the couch was about three million dollars they got from their bank robbery earlier in the day. By how it was laid out, they were in the midst of counting it.

"You little fools almost got shot. Better knock the next time you come home," Maggie said smirking.

Clyde turned to Maggie. "What you want us to do?"

She twisted her neck to get a clear view of Clyde's face. She couldn't believe what he had just asked. "Clyde, are you crazy? These are my kids, fool. Y'all drop them damn guns now."

The guns were dropped. Jupiter and Penny walked further inside and went over to the window. They stood quietly awaiting instructions on what to do next. Maggie looked at them in disgust.

"What's that under your arm?" she asked Jupiter, but looked directly at Penny. Penny was known as a blabber mouth, but Jupiter hoped this time she would be quiet.

"Momma, Jup won a big award. He's so smart," Penny said elated. "The mayor gave it to him."

"Penny..." Jupiter gave her an evil eye for opening up her mouth.

Maggie stared at him and at the award under his arm. "You weren't going to tell me about it? You better than me now? Don't forget you're only smart because of me."

"You gonna be somebody special one day my man. If you need anything, I got your back," Darius said, putting his hand on Jupiter's shoulder. "I mean that." He looked over at Maggie. "She loves you man."

Jupiter didn't respond. He did want to ask Clyde what ways his mother had shown this love because he hadn't seen it. It did make him feel good to hear encouragement from Clyde and Darius. He was surprised to receive such praise from them since they were ruthless criminals.

"We got you two some pizza over there and a couple of sodas. Keep up the good work." Clyde patted him on the back.

"Eat up," Darius said, shaking Jupiter's hand and slipping two hundred dollar bills in his hand. He immediately walked away.

Jupiter nodded and grabbed his sister and headed over to where the pizza was sitting. They ate the pizza hoping that no one noticed them.

"I'm not sure Justine deserves fifty percent of the take. We did all the work. I think we should go independent," Maggie said in protest. "I don't like it."

"You know Justine don't play when it comes to her money. You're her sister, but she won't care at all about taking us out. I like living," one of the guys sitting on the couch counting money said.

"You scared? Grow some balls. We have to split a million and a half four ways while she gets a whole million and half by herself. I'm tired of finishing last. We take the risk, and she gets the reward. I love her, but this has to change," Maggie said getting more upset just thinking about it.

"Man, Mags is right, we need a new deal. Justine won't touch us as long as Mags is on our side. I know I would like to keep a bigger share," Clyde said. "If we would have got caught today, we would have went to prison, not Justine. And knowing her, she would be saying that we still owe her."

"But Justine is the one giving us the layout and schedule. Without her help, we have nothing," Darius said. "Let's not ruin a good thing."

"I should shoot you now," Clyde said shaking his head at Darius.

"I'll talk to her tomorrow and see where her head is at. I think she will be agreeable to our way of thinking. My sister does love me. Plus, it's not as if we are cutting her out totally.

She will still get a cut." Maggie felt good about her chance of getting her sister to agree to some new terms.

"It's about time we get paid." Clyde laughed out loud. "Clyde likes slim change too."

Maggie looked at her kids who were still eating pizza. "I got hungry ass kids to feed. Slow down, save some for us smart ass. What's the square root of this apartment?" she said with laughter. "How was school today?"

"It was great," Penny said smiling at her mother.

Jupiter was tight lipped. He didn't look at his mother.

"You can't speak. How was your damn day? You won an award. Must have been good," Maggie shouted.

"It was okay," he replied back, hoping his mother wouldn't ask any more questions.

"Sorry I couldn't make it, but I'm trying to pay some bills around this piece. See that..." Maggie pointed at the money on the couch. "That's real work. That's the real world. I make money. Don't think you're ever better than me. Marion Barry graduated from your school too. See what happened to him?" She laughed.

"I know, Momma," Jupiter said.

"You better know." Maggie saw Clyde look at his watch. She also noticed that all the money was now back in the suitcases. "We are about to leave. I should be back before nine. Finish that pizza and do your homework. I don't want to get any bad reports from school about you. See you two later."

Maggie, Clyde, Darius, and the other guy packed up the money and the guns. They walked out the door. Once the door closed, Clyde turned to Maggie.

"I'm taking you to Vegas tonight," he said kissing her up against the wall.

"What about my kids?" she asked.

"You raising a genius in there. He can take care of himself and the little girl."

"Her name is Penny," Maggie said, knowing he forgot her name.

Clyde snapped his fingers as if to say 'I knew that'. "I knew it was something like that. So, are you in?"

Maggie looked back at the door. "When have I passed up a free trip? You know I'm in like Flynn. Okay, after we drop off the money, let's head to the airport."

"Whatever you say baby." Clyde kissed her. "We could triple our money."

"Yeah, our money, not my sister's," Maggie said slitting her eyes at him. She wanted him to understand that she wasn't gambling with her sister's money.

Clyde put up his hands. "You are so afraid of your sister."

"You don't know her like I do. She doesn't play with her money. Justine has multiple personalities and shit."

"I get it, she got crazy bitch syndrome. We go to Vegas and Clyde gonna triple his worth."

"I don't know if that's a good idea, Clyde. Justine doesn't like to play with the money," Maggie said.

Clyde ran his fingers through her hair. "I'm going to spoil your pretty ass in Vegas. I want to make love on a million."

Maggie giggled like a little school girl. "You know I love when you talk like Jay-Z."

"Come to Vegas, I'm gonna give you that hard knock life in the bed."

"Okay, but we got to come right back in the morning."

Clyde smiled. "Of course."

ॐ

The next day on the way to school, a black Brabus Mercedes Benz G 63 started following Jupiter after he dropped off Penny at school. At first, he pretended to not see the car and steadily walked down the street. Time went by and one block turned to five, he noticed that the car was still slowly following him. He approached the last block across the street from his school, and then out of the corner of his eye, he saw the car speed up and cut him off. Jupiter panicked and stood there wondering what they wanted. With all the windows being tinted, he couldn't see who was inside. He did have an idea that it had something to do with his mother. The backseat window came down. A black man sitting in the backseat wearing dark sunglasses smiled at him.

"I know you're not afraid of your Uncle Tony," the man said glaring at him menacingly.

Jupiter stared into the car with nervous tension. "Hi, Uncle Tony. I didn't know that was you."

Uncle Tony gave him a weird look. "You're not afraid of much are you?"

Jupiter looked at his watch. "I'm going to be late for school, Uncle Tony," he said.

Uncle Tony rolled his eyes. "Huh, you are such a nerd. I don't know who your daddy is, but damn, I know you do not take after your mother or anybody in my family."

Jupiter was antsy. He wanted to head to the school yard as he saw some of his classmates heading inside the school. "I don't want to be late."

"You gonna get hurt." Uncle Tony opened up the car door and got out. His six foot four and two hundred fifty pound muscular frame towered over Jupiter. "Where's your momma at?"

Jupiter looked up at him. "I don't know. I haven't seen her since last night after I got home from school."

Uncle Tony got real close in his face, almost nose to nose. "You know you better not be lying to me. I'll go after Penny."

His threat immediately got Jupiter's attention. "I told you I haven't seen her. Leave Penny out of this."

Uncle Tony laughed. "You love your sister, I see." Uncle Tony checked his watch and saw that it was near the school bell ringing time. "If you see your mother, tell her to do the smart thing. We're all family. I don't want to hurt my own sister. And you don't want to see me mad either."

Uncle Tony got back in the car and his driver took off. Once they were down the street from him, Jupiter raced across the street into school. As he walked inside, he wondered what kind of trouble his mother was in to have her brother looking for her. And by Uncle Tony's menacing look, he figured his intentions weren't good.

CHAPTER FOUR

L ater that same afternoon, Maggie and Clyde came back to her apartment, happy as can be. They were wearing high priced clothes, top of the line jewelry, and parked outside was a brand new red GLS 450 Mercedes Benz SUV that Clyde had just purchased. As they walked inside the apartment, they were quickly pounded into the floor with fists and baseball bats. When the beatings stopped, semi-automatic weapons were pointed in their faces.

Uncle Tony looked down at his sister with pity and shame. He was her little brother, and growing up he idolized his sisters, but always felt Maggie was something special. He now knew that it was just a mirage. It pained him to have to beat his own sister, but it was a part of the business when people screwed over Justine and the family.

"What the hell were you thinking?" he looked at Maggie on the verge of tearing up. Seeing the blood drip from her face and how she clutched her stomach made him feel uneasy.

Maggie's mouth was bloodied. She looked up at Uncle Tony with the only eye that could open. "We were going to bring the money today. You didn't have to do this."

"Mag, you know the rules. No one is above them. If you break the rules, then everybody will start breaking them. This is about respect."

"Man, we got her fuckin' money," Clyde said from the floor. "You want to start a war?"

Uncle Tony kicked him in the face. "Did anybody tell you to speak? ...I didn't think so."

"Tony, the money is at the drop. That's where we just came from," Maggie pleaded.

"Chico, make the call," Uncle Tony said, ordering one of his men to call and check Maggie's story. Chico quickly made the call. After about thirty seconds, Chico nodded over to Uncle Tony signaling that she was telling the truth.

Maggie struggled, but got to her feet. She looked her brother dead in his eyes. Anger steamed off of her as she pushed him in the chest. "Look at what you did to me." She pointed at her face. "I'm the one who brought you on. You backstabbing son of a bitch. We're through. You're going to need me before I need you. I know all your little dark secrets."

Uncle Tony turned away from her, but Maggie still slapped him.

He grabbed her by the arm. "You know this is what Justine ordered. I'm just following what she wanted me to do. You know she don't like him." Uncle Tony glanced down at Clyde.

"Let go of me." Maggie snatched her arm from him. "Clyde is with me. He's my problem, not hers."

"But...," Uncle Tony started to say.

"But nothing. I'm not analyzing who's in her bed." Maggie huffed. "Let's go talk to her right now."

"What time your kids come home?" Uncle Tony asked.

"Stay away from my damn kids Tony. I don't play that, you sick bastard."

"You need to stop trippin so much. They my family too."

Maggie slit her eyes at him. "So, I'm trippin? Now that's funny. You should be in jail or dead, you pervert."

"I'm just trying to make sure they are cared for when they come home," Uncle Tony said staring at her.

"They will be home at none of your fuckin' business, which is thirty minutes past you can kiss my ass. Let's just go."

∽

That afternoon when Jupiter and Penny were walking home, a bigger kid from their neighborhood came by on his bicycle. By Jupiter's tensed facial expression, you could tell he wasn't too fond of the boy. The bigger kid was a bully who had been a thorn in Jupiter's side for a while now.

"Where's your momma at, Jupiter? What kind of name is that anyway? Only a druggie names their kid a planet." The boy laughed to himself.

Jupiter ignored him as he and Penny continued to walk toward home. The boy was persistent and continued to follow them, which only annoyed Jupiter more.

"Your cousin Jabari said your mother is a whore. I got a buck for a fuck."

The boy's words struck a chord with him. Though his mother was a terrible person, she was still his mother. He had always defended her like she was innocent. Jupiter readied himself to strike if the boy said more.

"Just go. I don't want any trouble, man." Jupiter hoped that he'd ride off. The boy went nowhere. He rode his bike right next to them as they walked.

"I'm just trying to be cool with you. Everybody knows you and your sister are the freaks in the neighborhood." The boy cut in front of them and stopped his bike dead in their path. "Don't get hurt Mars." The boy laughed.

Without a pause, Jupiter dropped his school backpack and jumped on the boy. He punched him several times until the boy submitted. Though the boy screamed so that Jupiter would stop, he didn't. It wasn't until Penny told him to stop that did he listened to anything.

"I'm sorry. Just don't hit me anymore. The kids over there told me to come bother you, and they would give me ten dollars. I just want to go."

Jupiter got off the kid and stared down the street to the kids that the boy was referring to. He shook his head then showed his right fist. "I got more of this if they want to put up cash. Tell them to bring it."

The boy picked himself up and scampered off running, leaving his bike behind.

Jupiter put his backpack on and grabbed his sister's hand again, and they continued their walk home.

&

Over at Justine's house on Front Street, in the basement, Maggie walked into the plush home office full of rage. Right behind her was Clyde. Justine Jones sat at her desk anticipating a fight. Upon seeing her sister, they just stared, trying to intimidate the other. Justine was the oldest sister out of the three of them. She had an enticing beautiful smile, but in her eyes you could see that she held a dark, mysterious, cold hearted side. Justine was the mastermind behind the fortune her family had amassed. Her former boyfriend, who taught them the business, had died about ten years ago, and that's when the Jones's took control. Her organized crime family was the biggest in the state with connections all over the country and Mexico. She was the chief distributor of drugs and guns and headed the organized crime family called the Seven Fingers. The Seven Fingers consisted of

Justine's crew, The Gangster Disciples, Vice Lords, La Raza Nation, Crips, Bloods, and a group of Russians. Her power extended from the highest of government officials to the lowest scumbag crawling out from under a rock. If she wanted something done or someone dead, it happened. Outside of those knowledgeable, few knew the cold blooded killer and business woman that she was. She lived in a house that was four stories and did have eight bedrooms, ten baths, a media/game room, and a pool on the rooftop. She housed twelve people. While reflecting wealth, it still didn't communicate that she was worth over six hundred million dollars. To the public at large, Justine was just another foster parent in the system, but to the politicians and officers on the payroll, she was a feared woman capable of every sinister act known to man.

"Look at what you did to me?" Maggie shouted. "You gonna pay for this!"

Justine motioned for her to lower her voice. Maggie huffed, but did.

"What were you thinking taking off to Vegas with my money?" Justine snarled. "This is business."

"So, you thought I was going to steal from us and run to Vegas?" Maggie laughed. "Are you hearing yourself right now? So, you don't trust me? I'm your sister. I was there for you when you had nothing."

"That's not the point. Maggie, you have been getting out of control lately. I told you, you need to seek some help."

"I got it under control. But when shit like this happens, it definitely makes me want to use something." Maggie glared at her.

Justine got up from her desk and walked around to the front of it. She leaned back on her desk. "I'm sorry, but we have protocols to follow and you broke them. And I know you did it for this piece of shit next to you."

"Who you calling a piece of shit, bitch!" Clyde said before Uncle Tony and some of the other guards grabbed him. "If it wasn't for me the Disciples wouldn't be a part of this. You owe me."

"I owe you a bullet in the head. The Disciples are with us now," Uncle Tony said choking Clyde around his neck. "They don't care about you."

Justine looked at Maggie and shook her head. Maggie wanted to help Clyde, but in this case it wasn't a good idea to do that, so she just stood there. Justine went over and grabbed Uncle Tony's gun from him. It was like she flipped a switch in her head, and her smile disappeared. Her face held an evil scowl. She then shot Clyde in the leg. He dropped to the floor in excruciating pain.

"Call me a bitch again, and I'm putting one in your head. Clyde, nobody will miss you. My sister will get over you very soon. I would suggest that you learn some respect because you ain't no Jesus, and you will not be resurrected. You're nothing."

Clyde stood there fighting off the pain and the tears. He looked over at Maggie, hoping that she would say something. She didn't.

Justine turned her attention back to her sister. "Where are my niece and nephew at?"

"Should be at home. Why?"

Surprisingly, Justine went and gave Maggie a hug. Maggie didn't know what was going on as the gun pressed up against her back. Justine pulled away from her. She looked in Maggie's face and forced a smile.

"You have those kids living like POW hostages. I have ears everywhere. I don't like hearing about them at home by themselves with nothing to eat. The heat turned off and you putting them in the hallway so you can screw some loser." She glanced over at Clyde. "With all the money you've made, you still live like an alley rat in a sewer. Just because you're a rat doesn't mean you treat your kids that way."

"Who told you that stuff?" Maggie asked getting paranoid. "Jupiter!"

Justine slit her eyes. "I haven't talked to my extremely smart nephew in months. He's going places. You know the Mayor came to his school to personally give him an award. The other day, I told the Mayor that he was my people, and he couldn't believe it. Now, why would the Mayor of our great city tell me that Jupiter's mother didn't show up for this event and that he was told that she never shows up for anything and is a drug head. You're embarrassing me. I hope you're not hooked on that fish scale or meth?"

Maggie got tight lipped. Her thoughts were consumed with knowing who could be watching her that closely. Justine saw her thinking hard about it.

"Don't blow your brains out trying to figure out my sources." Justine chuckled. She looked down at her watch. "Is there anything else we need to discuss?"

Maggie looked over at Clyde. "No."

"You can take my old Altima home. The limo is being detailed. I'll have someone come get it later. Make sure he doesn't bleed on my carpets. That car is special, it reminds me of where I come from." Justine walked back over to her chair and sat back down. "Make sure next time you drop off my money before you go partying. And tell that nigga to do better than Vegas next time. Think outside the box. Vegas is for low breeding Americans and foreigners who don't know real ballin'."

Maggie was almost out the door when she turned back around. "I want a better deal. We take all the risk, but you get just as much as us. Let's be fair."

Justine stared at everyone in the room. She knew this was a critical challenge that she needed to address. "You do realize that I'm being very fair. I give you the layout, provide you the guns, get the inside connections to help with bank protocols, and give you the damn getaway cars. And you think me getting half is unfair?"

"Yeah, bring your ass to the bank and let's see what happens then."

Justine quickly ran her fingers through her long black hair. "Let me tell you something, sister. You're lucky that I haven't killed him yet. If it wasn't for you, he would have had slow singing and flower bringing a long time ago. He's a loser and he's corrupting your brain. You're going down a dangerous road. I love you, but if you want to go down with him, I will make it happen. I'm sure the mortuary will give me a two death discount."

"So, you want to kill me?" Maggie asked.

"If I have too, I will. This is bigger than you and me. This is about the Seven Fingers Organization. No one will bring down this dynasty." Justine waved them off to leave her presence.

Maggie walked out of the basement office with Clyde limping beside her. They were both pissed off and, by the grimace on their faces, they wished Justine's downfall was today. No matter what was said, they still felt Justine was being unfair in their deal.

CHAPTER FIVE

S ix months had gone by since Maggie had her showdown with Justine. The showdown made Maggie paranoid. With her knowing that Justine was spying, she made a concerted effort to change some of her negative ways, especially in her parenting. The biggest change was that she didn't leave Jupiter and Penny at home alone and kept the refrigerator filled with food. To her surprise, the change also brought her closer to her kids. Maggie started liking being their mother. Her change was peculiar and shocking to Jupiter and Penny too. Jupiter and Penny wondered what was behind it, but were too afraid to ask.

On Union Avenue, between Manassas Street and Marshall Avenue, Clyde was sitting in his red Mercedes Benz SUV across from SunTrust Bank, casing it out. Maggie jumped back in the car and started explaining the security guard situation, how many tellers were working, and if the vault was open. Once she mentioned the vault being opened, Clyde's eyes grew big.

"This seems like an easy job. We could take it right now," he said with one eye on Maggie. He wanted to know what she thought.

"Does seem easy, but Justine wants us to hit it next week on Thursday."

Clyde rubbed the leg that Justine had shot. "Forget her. I say we take it right now. She can't get a cut if we're not using anything from her."

"What about the getaway car Clyde?"

"Clyde got this car right here, baby," Clyde said grinning.

"I can't. I got to pick up my kids from school." Maggie said. Going against the schedule to rob a bank spontaneously wasn't how they normally had done things. Plus she thought back to the last time they crossed paths with Justine.

Clyde kissed her. "This is our opportunity to be our own people. We can be the boss now. Fuck Justine!"

"Can't you be happy with what you already have?" Maggie had a bad feeling about reneging from the deal she had with her sister.

"While somebody is raping me? Hell naw! I want the good life too."

"What do you want from me, Clyde?" Maggie asked.

Clyde grabbed her by the hand. "I just want you for once to follow me, listen to me, and let me be the leader. I promise you, you won't regret it."

She looked into his eyes. "You think we can take this today?"

"Clyde knows his banks," Clyde said winking at her. "You said the vault was open and that they only got two security guards working. We can take this by ourselves."

"So now, we're Bonnie and Clyde?"

Clyde smiled. "We can be."

Maggie saw the seriousness in his eyes. "So, if we don't have another car then how do we get away?" Maggie didn't understand his plan.

"That's where you come in. We pick up your kids from school and park in front of the bank."

"Are you crazy?" She thought what he was suggesting was outrageous and stupid.

"Mags, that's the perfect cover. Nobody would expect us to rob a bank and drive off with kids." Clyde pulled out some fish scale cocaine. Maggie's eyes grew. She was craving it. The last six months she had been clean.

"I don't know. What if they shoot at us? My kids will be in the car."

"Everybody ducks. Have we ever been shot? Have we ever not gotten away? We'll pick up your kids and get them some ice cream. We will be in and out of the bank in two minutes tops. And we won't have to split anything." Clyde cut up the fish scale and snorted a line. He passed it on to Maggie. At first she just stared at it. Every fiber in her body said no to the fish scale and his plan, but there was something about him that controlled her. Clyde was the real drug that made her weak.

"It's still her plan," Maggie said to deter him. In her intense eyes, it was obvious that she was trying to fend off Clyde's pull on her.

Clyde smirked. "She owes us. She shot me for nothing. We'll give her ten percent for her plan, but nothing more." He kissed Maggie. "You're the love of my life."

"Okay baby, I'm in," she said taking her own snort and melting in front of him.

Clyde smiled at her.

⁂

About an hour later, Clyde, Maggie, Jupiter, and Penny were sitting in the car across from the same SunTrust Bank. Penny and Jupiter both were enjoying their ice cream, though Jupiter was leery of why his mother and Clyde had picked them up in the first place. Though their relationship with Maggie had improved, Jupiter was well aware of the great and deadly influence that Clyde had over her.

Clyde winked at Maggie. Jupiter saw it in the rearview mirror. He assumed something was about to occur.

"I got to go in the bank real quick to get some money out for us. Big night for us all," Clyde said as he opened up his door and popped the hatchback of his SUV.

"I need to check my account too. Jupiter you stay in this car until I come back. Okay?"

Jupiter thought her comment was absurd. Being about ten miles from home, why would he get out of the car to do anything, especially walk.

"Yeah, we'll be right here," he said, wondering what Clyde and his mother were up to. He had a sick sense that they were up to no good. He knew his mother was a criminal but was never told what her specialty actually was. "I'll be right back," Maggie said exiting the car.

Penny saw the concerned look on Jupiter's face. "Is everything okay Jupiter?" she asked, continuing to lick her ice cream cone.

He smiled. "Yeah Penny. Mommy and Clyde are going to make a withdrawal."

"How much money are they withdrawing?" Penny asked excited. "I want more chocolate ice cream.

"More than what they have in the bank."

Penny sat there trying to understand what he meant. "I don't understand."

"Penny, don't worry about it, we'll be home very soon," he said contemplating jumping out of the SUV with Penny and leaving.

It was about two minutes later, when Jupiter noticed the police officers at the bank doors with their guns drawn. He knew, at that point, he and Penny were now without a mother. He stared at his sister wanting to say something, but no words came from him. The ringing thought in his head was now he had to officially become the head of his family. With so many cops surrounding the bank and near the SUV, he knew they wouldn't make it far without being noticed by the police. Jupiter felt it was best to stay put and hope that no one saw them.

On the opposite side of the bank, Maggie and Clyde were walking out into the alley. They felt trapped. Both of them stared at the other. This was the first time they had ever been cornered. They feared the worst. Out of the corner of her eye, Maggie saw the manhole, but didn't want to say anything. She knew exactly what Clyde would say once she told him.

"Clyde, what about my kids?" she said in anguish.

Clyde looked at her like she was crazy. "What about us? We're trapped. If we go down to the end of that alley we're toast. If we go back in that bank were dead. Clyde ain't going back to prison."

"My kids are over there waiting for us." Maggie was in tears. "I made a mistake. It wasn't supposed to be like this."

"What do you think is going to happen if you go over there to get your kids? You think the cops are going to be like 'we understand, take your kids and the money'? You're going to prison, and your kids are going in the system. No matter how you look it, it comes down to you either wanting your freedom or wanting to be locked up. This has nothing to do with your kids now."

Maggie hated to admit it, but Clyde was somewhat right. There was no silver lining to this story. No matter how it played out, she and her kids were not going to be together. The thought of them being stuck in the system hurt her deeply. Though she hadn't been the best mother, lately she had started to believe she could be the mother they needed. Now, with the cops closing in, that dream was slipping away fast. Saving herself was the top priority now.

"There's a manhole over there. I saw it on the map. It leads out to the docks. We can go from there and get on a plane to anywhere before the police know who did it," she said gritting her teeth.

"That's a game plan I'm down with. My baby is smart." Clyde smiled.

Clyde went and opened up the manhole. He threw the three huge bags filled with money down first and then he went. Half way down he yelled, "You coming, right?"

Maggie took one final look and ran over to join him. Shortly after she closed the manhole, the police came to the alley, clueless about where they might have gone. None of the officers noticed the manhole until it was too late. They opened it and saw nothing. The officers couldn't believe Maggie and Clyde had disappeared that easily.

CHAPTER SIX

A s the police cleared out the bank and started their manhunt for Clyde and Maggie, Jupiter and Penny remained in the back seat. Jupiter knew leaving earlier might have been smart, but now they had to hope that nobody noticed them waiting. That hope ended quickly as an officer saw them in the backseat. Luckily, Jupiter did get a chance to grab the old beat up looking notebook that Maggie had under the passenger seat before the officer approached the SUV. The officer carefully looked in. Seeing that they were kids and unarmed, he opened the door.

"Who are you waiting on?" the officer asked.

Penny was about to talk until Jupiter stopped her. "Penny, you don't talk to strangers."

"I'm sorry. I'll be quiet now," she said to the officer.

The officer grew angry at Jupiter. "Now son, you really don't want to not talk to me. Do you want to spend a night in jail?"

"You can't arrest me! I didn't do anything wrong."

The officer angrily stared at him. "I can make your life very difficult. Who are you waiting on?" To him, all signs pointed to this being the getaway car.

Jupiter frowned. "My uncle Clyde told us to wait in the car while he went to make a withdrawal. Is he coming?"

"Was he alone? The witnesses say that he was with a woman. Do you know who the woman might have been?"

Jupiter shook his head innocently. He knew the officer was trying to catch him in a lie. "No sir. He picked us up from school today and drove us here. Did something happen to my uncle Clyde?"

"Who do you live with?" the officer asked.

"Uncle Clyde," Jupiter said holding his emotions together. "Is he dead?"

"No. Where's your mother?"

"She's been out of town for a while. We haven't seen her in a couple of months."

"Why not? Does she work out of town?" Jupiter's coy responses frustrated the officer.

"No sir, I don't think she's ever coming back," he said sadly, knowing that he was probably speaking the truth.

"Okay, come with me. I'll take you downtown, and we'll figure out where you can go. Are there any other relatives?"

"No," Jupiter said as he and Penny got out of the car. While they walked to the patrol car, Jupiter looked around wondering what happened to his mother.

Penny whispered to him. "Why did you lie to the police officer?"

He placed his index finger over his mouth. "If I told the truth Mommy would be in a lot of trouble," he whispered back to her.

"But she didn't do anything wrong?"

Jupiter was speechless as they got into the backseat of the patrol car.

❧

In a stolen car, Clyde and Maggie headed toward the Memphis International Airport. They had changed clothes and were dressed like business people heading to work. Maggie was pissed at herself for leaving her kids but knew there wasn't any way for them to ever be together again without her going to jail first. As they were pulling into the airport parking lot, her phone rang. She stared at it and let it go straight to voice mail, but it rang again. And again.

Clyde looked over at her. "Answer it, it doesn't matter now."

Maggie took a deep breath. "Hello."

"What the hell you do?" Justine yelled through the phone. "Clyde is dead."

"What are you talking about?" Maggie said.

Justine huffed. "You think I'm stupid to not know you robbed that bank today? Maggie, I thought you were better than this. I told you that man and those drugs would be the death of you, but I lied, it's going to be me. I am going to hunt you and him down and hang you. Then I will burn your body in the garbage like regular trash because that's all you are now to me, regular trash."

Maggie gritted her teeth. She was fed up with her sister's threats. "You have never scared me. Like I said, I don't know what you're talking about. If you want a war with me then go for it. I'll get you before you get me."

"So, what are you going to do about your kids at the police station? They were found outside of the bank in the back seat of Clyde's car. Big red SUV parked across the street from the bank. How stupid are you?"

Maggie was stuck. She thought about what her sister had just said and agreed that it was a stupid plan from the beginning. But she wasn't about to tell her sister that. Maggie didn't say a word for several seconds as she thought about what to say.

"What are you going to do?" Justine repeated with anger.

"You better not hurt my kids," Maggie yelled into the phone.

"Somebody has to pay for your sins; it sure won't be Jesus."

"Justine, I swear I will kill you. This is between you and me, not my kids." Maggie started to cry. "You put one scratch on them and ..."

"You gonna do what? Run Maggie run. That's what you do best," Justine said.

"Justine..."

Justine smiled as she got out of her limousine near the police station. "I'm waiting for you at the police station. Come on down, sister."

Maggie didn't know what to do, so she hung up the phone and broke it and tossed it away.

"What she say?" Clyde asked knowing that it couldn't have been good.

"We need to go back," she said adamantly. "She's going to make my kids pay for this."

"We can't. You want to go to jail?"

"Give me the car keys. That witch is going to hurt my kids. I can't allow that," Maggie said determined to go back.

Clyde saw the sad, long face she held. Though he was self-absorbed with his own survival, he understood her plight. "Baby, it's nothing you can do now. You gonna go back and get your kids and do what? Go to jail? Then what have you done? Your kids are either going to a foster home or with Justine. You can't save them Maggie. I'm sorry. I wish there was another way."

"I got to do something." Maggie said. "They don't deserve this."

Clyde gave her a strange glare. "Why you care now?"

Maggie looked off into the empty air. "I should've cared a long time ago. They my kids, Clyde," she said, desperately wanting to go back.

"Hey, it's too late now. What's real is I got us to two tickets to Rio. I got some friends there that will look out for us. When we get there, we will think it through. I can't wait any longer neither can you." Clyde got out of the car.

Maggie sat there sulking as Clyde stood outside. She cried and said a silent prayer, hoping for her kids to be safe then got out of the car herself.

"When is Darius sending our money to Brazil?"

Clyde smiled. "Today. He's boxing it up and sending it through FedEx. Within two days we will have our money. It's going to be wonderful." Clyde walked over to her and grabbed her hand. He stared in her eyes. "Clyde loves you baby."

Maggie couldn't get the thought of her kids being with Justine out of her mind, but knew that there was nothing she could do at this point.

"Let's just get out of here," she said, rushing them along as she fought off the tears.

∽

At the precinct, Justine sat across from Jupiter and Penny. Jupiter could tell by the menacing look on his aunt's face that she was not pleased by something. He noticed the multiple times that she clutched and balled up her fist while speaking with them and the officers. When the officers walked away, Jupiter decided to speak.

"Penny, go sit over there for a minute. I need to talk to Auntie," he said.

Justine wondered what he had to say to her. Jupiter waited until Penny was out of earshot before speaking again.

He turned his attention back to his aunt. "Where is our mother?" he asked staring at her.

Justine stared coldly back at him. "Your mother is never coming to get you. You think she cares about you?"

"And you do?" he said back to her. "We barely know you."

"I'm here. She's not. What choice do you have?"

Jupiter saw the emerging anger grow in her eyes. He always knew Justine was dangerous by the respect everyone paid her. The relationship between her and them had been almost non-existent. The few times they did interact Justine had been pleasant. Not wanting to appear scared, he didn't flinch while staring back at her. He figured by what she had just said that his mother had crossed her for the last time, and she wanted to use them to find her.

"So what about us?" He figured she hadn't come out of the woodwork before to check on them. And if not then, why now? Jupiter wanted to fully understand her angle.

Justine was impressed by his not backing down. "You are a smart kid. I don't know how such a dumb woman could have such a smart child. Maybe your daddy was Einstein," she said with a chuckle. "What do you want to happen?"

"I just want to go home with my sister. We don't need anybody."

Justine smiled. "You don't have that luxury."

"You're not my mother." Jupiter held his ground.

"You never had a mother. Let me lay it down for you. You're fourteen years old, she's seven, and have no home or parent. If you can find your daddy then great, but you would have a better chance winning the lottery. Your choices are simple. Come with me or go into the system. I'm all you got."

"I'll go into the system."

"You're right, you will go into the system," Justine said looking over at Penny. "She's coming with me. And there's nothing you can do about that."

"I'll..."

Justine tilted her head to the side. "You going to threaten me. Now that's tough. I might have a place for you in the future. Don't cross me, or that place becomes a grave."

"I don't want to work for you," he angrily brushed off her offer.

"Look around, everybody works for me." Justine shook her head at him. "When the officer comes back, you are going to tell him that you want to live with your aunt, and we're going to go home. You're going to be one of my foster kids. I'm going to get money from the state for you and her."

"Why are you doing this?" he asked. "You don't need the money."

"You're mother got bills to pay, and you're my collateral."

Before Jupiter could respond, the officer came back over to them.

"Miss Jones, I don't see any reason why these kids can't go home with you. Jupiter, do you see a reason for me to not let you go home with your aunt?" the officer asked.

"I..." Jupiter looked her in the eyes. "No, my sister and I would love to be with our aunt. She's like a second mother."

"But officer, I will need to put them in my foster home. Just like I have with my other kids."

"No problem. Keep up the good work, Miss Jones." The officer winked at her.

"Thanks," Justine said. "Penny, come over here. You and your brother are coming home with me. We're a family now."

Jupiter stared at Justine while Penny went to her and gave her a hug. Justine turned and stared right back at him. Jupiter knew this situation was far from over. He figured his aunt's intentions were marred with revenge against his mother. How he and his sister figured into those plans were a complete mystery to him.

CHAPTER SEVEN

When they left the precinct and got into the limousine parked out front, Justine wanted to get Jupiter and Penny straight on how things would be now that they would be living with her. Her attitude was more for Jupiter because she saw him as a person who thought independently and did what he wanted, whereas, most of the people surrounding her did what she wanted, no questions asked.

Justine leaned forward and stared both of them in the face. "Now, I want to make something very clear. You are my sister's children and I like you, but don't cross me. I will do whatever it takes to pay you back. And I'm telling you now, what happens at my house better not get out. If I hear one thing about what I do come out of your mouth then I will make an example of you in front of everyone living in my house."

Jupiter raised his hand to speak.

"And you only speak when told. I own you now," Justine said as Jupiter lowered his hand. "And don't get any bright ideas. I have a lot of friends in high and low places that will do the strangest things like separate the two of you, which I wouldn't want to do." She smiled. "But it's a possibility."

"Can I speak Auntie?" Penny asked, looking over at Jupiter.

"Of course baby," Justine said. She thought about giving Penny the riot act for interrupting her but decided not to.

Justine did like Penny and wished that she was her own daughter. Justine never had children for the fear of creating a weakness for herself. She had her tubes tied at twenty-one. She trusted no one. To her, fear and money had been more important than love.

"I don't want to be apart from Jupiter. He's my only brother. I love him." Penny's eyes watered up.

This touched Justine's heart just enough to have her say, "I want you to stay together, but that depends on your brother."

Penny grabbed his hand tightly and gave him puppy dog eyes. "Jupiter, make sure we stay together," Penny said pleading to her brother.

Justine stared over at him. She nodded, giving Jupiter the okay to speak. He hated the predicament that they were in. He wished they could bolt out of the limousine and run, but they had no home or food, and definitely no money. For Penny's sake, he was willing to do whatever it took for them to stay together as a family.

"Penny, we'll always be together, that's my promise. We're a team. I got your back," Jupiter said with confidence. "It's going to be good living at Auntie's house.

❧

That night right after they settled in their new house, Jupiter started reading Maggie's notebook. He saw that she had been jotting down notes and poems for years. Based on the dates that she put in the notebook, she had begun about twenty years ago. He remembered seeing her write in it, but never knew what she was writing. Since they really didn't communicate that much, he thought it was typical criminal garbage. But once he started reading, he discovered a different person than the woman he knew as his mother. It blew his mind that she created such beautiful poetry and stories. He saw her intelligence written between the lines and had an awkward appreciation for the woman he barely knew.

In her writing, he saw where some of his talents had come from. But as he read, Jupiter noticed a man's name that she mentioned over and over as the love of her life; Marcellus J. Carpenter. Midway through the notebook, he found out that Marcellus was his father. That unearthing led him to be even more curious to find out who Penny's father was. He read feverishly throughout the night until he got to the crushing news that Penny's father had raped Maggie and had died in a car accident. After reading that information, he almost put the book down, but he was too eager to finish and went to her last entry. It was a poem. He smiled then read it out loud softly to not wake up Penny, lying in the next bed.

"They probably hate me and should. I hate myself for not being the mother that would walk through fire for my offspring. I hate who I am and who I be. They are angels being raised by the devil within me. I brought them into the world, a handsome boy and a beautiful little girl, and I failed them. Instead of nurturing, I've been torturing; instead of uplifting I've been drifting. I wish I could erase my mistakes, but a life of crime seems to be my fate. I hate that they will probably have my same fate unless, by the grace of a higher power, they are saved, and the ankle weights from my sins are turned into fins, and they can swim away."

A couple of tears fell from his eyes, and he wiped them away. Jupiter closed the notebook and fell to sleep.

∽

The next morning came swiftly, but, like every other day in his young life, Jupiter woke up, took a shower, got dressed, and did the same for his sister. As they were walking out of the house, his Uncle Tony approached him from behind. It startled him.

"Hold up young buck," Uncle Tony said grabbing him by the shoulder.

Jupiter pulled away and turned around to face him. He didn't like his uncle much and knew whatever he wanted wouldn't be to his liking.

"We gonna be late. We gotta go," he said hoping Uncle Tony would just leave him alone.

Uncle Tony waved off his words as nonsense. "I'm not trying to hear that garbage. I need you to drop something off to somebody."

"Does Auntie know about this?" Jupiter asked. "How come Jabari can't do it?"

His questions only pissed off Uncle Tony even more. Uncle Tony snatched him up by the front shirt collar. "You're a puppy barking up a big tree, don't get hit by that large branch." Uncle Tony raised his fist up at Jupiter. "Let's make this clear right now. When I give you an order, don't you dare question me. Just do it!"

Jupiter's face showed his fear. He had always been afraid of his uncle. His uncle had been the muscle of the family and had murdered a multitude of people. Uncle Tony was a feared man in the city and known for many crazy acts of violence and deviant sexual behaviors.

"I'm sorry," Jupiter said in a low voice. "I just need to get to school."

"You are such a nerd. You're a disgrace to this family. Grow some. We only need soldiers around here."

Jupiter just stared at him.

"I guess you too smart to listen to me," Uncle Tony said chuckling. He handed a note to Jupiter and handed him a duffle bag filled with drugs.

Jupiter started to sweat knowing what was in the bag and that he had to carry this around. "Do I have to?" He asked.

"You got to pay for your stay here. No free rides. Take it to the liquor store across the street from your school at three o'clock. You get out at 2:45, right?"

"Yeah," Jupiter replied.

"That's what I want to hear. Since you're running late, I'll have the limo take you to school this morning. My gift."

"Where's Jabari at?" Jupiter asked.

Uncle Tony grinned at him. "My son is just like me in one aspect, he doesn't trust your ass or like you. He got his own car. He ain't trying to be seen with you."

Jupiter stood there steaming.

Another little girl, about eight years old, came down the stairs and went into the kitchen. Uncle Tony blew a kiss at her, which Jupiter saw and looked at Penny. He grabbed her, and they quickly went outside. Walking toward the limousine, he stopped and looked at her.

"Penny, I don't want you to get anywhere near Uncle Tony. You have to promise me that," he said with deep sincerity.

"Okay, but why? Uncle Tony is nice to me."

Her response wasn't good enough for Jupiter. "Penny, just promise me. Stay away from him please."

She saw the concern in his eyes. "Why Jupiter?"

He raised his voice. "Penny, stay away from him. Promise me now?"

"Okay, I promise."

"I have to keep you safe. Don't you want us to stay together?" he asked.

"Yeah," Penny replied confused by why he didn't want her to talk to Uncle Tony.

He gave her a big hug. "We're going to make it out of here. I promise you that. Just listen to me, and we'll be alright. I love you, Penny."

"I love you too Jupiter," she said giving him a kiss on the cheek.

"Let's go have a good day at school," Jupiter said as he grabbed her hand and led her toward the limousine.

∽

The school day had been an uncomfortable and torturous one for Jupiter. He was distracted by the duffle bag filled with drugs in his locker. He prayed more than ever that day, but it didn't help. No one appeared to save him.

The other thing that consumed him was his research on Marcellus J. Carpenter. He searched the internet at school during every break he had until he found who he thought was the right person. The address he found was in Oakland, California. Out of curiosity, he also looked up Penny's father and saw that the car accident had been ruled a homicide. With this new information, he dreamt that life with his father would be great if he could only meet him.

Jupiter noticed that it was two forty. His heart pounded. With five minutes to go, his anxiety only rose. He wanted to get the drop over with successfully so that his aunt and uncle might leave him and Penny alone and not have him work to pay off his mother's debt. Though he dismissed it, in the back of his mind, Jupiter wondered if this was just the beginning of his end.

"Is everything alright, Mr. Jones?" Jupiter's teacher asked, noticing his awkward behavior. "You haven't seemed like yourself today."

Jupiter looked around at his classmates who were staring at him. "I'm good. Have to do something for my mom after school." He glanced up at the wall clock again. It was now two forty three.

His teacher stared at him for a second, wondering if he was lying or not. "Okay. Everyone make sure you get all of your homework done for tomorrow."

The school bell rang, and the students bolted out of the door. Jupiter slowly walked out of the classroom and to his locker. He was very nervous about opening up his locker with the other kids next to him. After a long mental debate, and seeing that it was now five minutes to three, he snatched the bag out of his locker and headed toward the school exit.

At the exit door, a black kid wearing a football letterman jacket walked up on him. It was his cousin, Jabari. Jabari stood six feet tall, about two inches taller than Jupiter, and weighed around two hundred thirty pounds. Without any equivocation, Jabari hated Jupiter. He was Lex Luther to Jupiter's Superman status. He was a year older, but being that Jupiter had skipped a grade, they were in the same grade. Throughout his life, all Jupiter ever heard was how smart his cousin was and how he would be the first from the family to graduate from college. He lived primarily with his mother, but spent a lot of time with his father to build street cred.

"What's up little bitch?" Jabari said brushing hard up against him.

Jupiter glared at him, wanting to sock him in the mouth. "Leave me alone."

Jabari stepped in his path. "You ain't shit!!"

Jupiter shoved his way past his cousin and went out the door.

As Jupiter walked off the school grounds, he kept looking over his shoulders, thinking that somebody had to know what he was about to do. This was one of the scariest moments in his life. When he crossed the street, he saw a man in his early twenties standing out in front of the liquor store. He walked over to the man.

"Are you Barry?" Jupiter asked, looking at the piece of paper that Uncle Tony had given.

"Who wants to know?" Barry asked as he placed one hand inside his coat pocket.

Jupiter glanced around. "I'm here for Uncle Tony."

Barry laughed. "Oh snap, you're the little dude. Okay, hold on for a second, I need to get that for you."

Barry left Jupiter and went around the back of the liquor store and quickly came back with a backpack. He handed it over to Jupiter. Jupiter didn't know what to do next.

"Hand it over kid," Barry demanded with his hand stretched out.

Jupiter gave him the other bag. "Thank you sir."

"What you call me?" Barry said. "You're different than the other kids."

"Okay, sir."

Barry smiled. "You are definitely a different type of kid. Tell Uncle Tony I'll get him the rest later."

"Okay," Jupiter said as he scampered away with the backpack.

∾

At four thirty, Jupiter and Penny arrived back at their aunt's house. Uncle Tony was waiting at the door. Jupiter fretted. Though their dislike for each other was apparent, Jupiter knew he needed to make nice with him in order for him and Penny to survive.

"Penny, when we get inside, go straight to our room and wait for me, Okay?"

Penny nodded. Uncle Tony opened the door for them. Penny had listened and went directly to their room.

"Where's my package?" Uncle Tony asked.

Jupiter handed him the backpack and walked by. Uncle Tony looked inside and counted the money with his eyes quickly.

"You better stop. We a little short, partner," Uncle Tony said .

Jupiter stopped. Uncle Tony stomped over to him and pushed him up against the wall.

"Where's my money?" he asked, getting nose to nose with him.

"That's what he gave me. He said to tell you he will have the rest later."

Uncle Tony chuckled. "Do I look like Visa? We don't give people credit around here. No money, no product. That's simple math, Einstein. You owe me fifty thousand dollars."

"I didn't know," Jupiter said with his mouth wide open.

"Or you didn't care? I bet you would care more if I put that ass on the streets."

Jupiter huffed. "You shouldn't have had me do it in the first place. Nobody told me what to do."

"You want to eat, sleep, and live, this is your damn job," Uncle Tony said growing angrier. "I want my fifty large."

"I'm sorry," Jupiter said as he turned to head to his room. "You know I don't have it."

"Sorry, I'll show you sorry."

Uncle Tony grabbed Jupiter by the neck and slammed him to the floor. He hit him several times in the face and kicked him in the ribs before some of the other adults living in the house pulled him off.

"You better go back tomorrow and either get my money or my product back or it's only going to get worst for you."

From the ground, Jupiter could see the other foster kids, Jabari, and Penny looking down at him from the second floor.

CHAPTER EIGHT

T he next afternoon, Jupiter shot out of school. Even though he was scared, not getting the money from Barry was not an option. There was no doubt in his mind that Uncle Tony would make his life a living hell if he came back empty handed. Like lightning, he ran to the liquor store, but didn't see Barry anywhere. Then out of the blue, Barry came up from behind him.

"What you doing back here, little proper dude?" Barry asked with a smirk.

"I need to get the rest of the money or the stuff back," Jupiter said with desperation in his voice. He stared at Barry with puppy dog eyes hoping to get his sympathy.

"That's not going to happen," Barry said dismissing him. "Tell Uncle Tony next week."

"That's not going to work. Uncle Tony wants his money now. He said no credit. Please give it to me," Jupiter begged.

Barry rolled his eyes. He could care less about Jupiter's problems. "Run on before something bad happens to you. This ain't a playground for kids."

Jupiter thought about his words and wanted to turn away and go home. It was already clear to him what would happen at home was going to be worse than what could happen to him at that moment.

"I can't," he said to Barry. "I need that money."

Barry punched him in the face. "You better get on. Don't make me hurt you."

Blood dripping from his nose, Jupiter stood his ground. "I can't. I need that money."

Jupiter took several more punches from Barry. He fell to the ground and remembered the look on Penny's face from yesterday. He quickly got up and ran away.

"You better get outta here," Barry said with confidence as he pulled out his gun. "You almost got shot."

As Jupiter was running off, he saw Uncle Tony's car down the street. He knew now that if he didn't get the money or product back that he might not make it back home. Jupiter changed his direction and went to the gas station down the street.

Inside the gas station, Jupiter got some matches and lighter fluid. When he went back down by the liquor store, his nerves were so bad that he vomited. He stopped about a half block away and waited on Barry to turn his back to him. He ran over to Barry and quickly squirted as much of the lighter fluid as possible on Barry's backside and legs. He then threw a match on him.

By the time Barry turned around, he saw Jupiter and the flames on his body. Jupiter snatched Barry's backpack off of his back and ran. Barry grabbed his gun and started shooting at Jupiter as he chased him around the liquor and in between the parked cars. When Jupiter heard that he was out of bullets, he looked over and saw Barry desperately trying putting out the fire on him.

Though in severe pain, he tried his best to stay strong, but once he heard his gun click over and over again with no bullets in the chamber, he fell to the ground. Jupiter ran over and commenced to beating Barry down with all his force. He didn't want to kill Barry but wanted to send him a message just in case they crossed paths again. It wasn't until he saw that Barry was unconscious and his fist was bleeding that Jupiter stopped.

Out the corner of his eyes, Jupiter caught a glimpse of Uncle Tony's car way down the street again. He knew Uncle Tony would take whatever was in the bag, but Jupiter didn't want him to get more than what he deserved. After he picked himself up, he ran down the alley and then cut through a couple of yards and back down another alley then stopped to check if the coast was clear. Seeing no one, Jupiter opened the bag. Inside he saw more money than he had ever possessed. He quickly counted it twice. He remembered yesterday Uncle Tony saying he better get his fifty thousand dollars back. Jupiter had counted eighty five thousand, and took the extra thirty thousand. He didn't know where he was going to hide it. Jupiter looked around and saw no place to put the money. His eyes welled up with tears. He wanted to hold on to the thirty thousand in hopes of having money for him and Penny to live on after they escaped.

"I got to put this money somewhere." Then he saw a sewer drain in the alley. He opened it and went down. Jupiter had a small pocket flashlight he used to navigate in the sewer.

"Auntie's house is that way. There has to be a hiding place down here." He walked for about ten minutes and then realized that he was walking on dirt. Jupiter stopped and started digging with his hands. He dug a hole about two feet deep within a matter of minutes. He took all of his books out of his backpack and placed the thirty thousand in it. He then put the bag in the hole and covered it back up. He stomped the ground several times to make it seem normal. He used his flashlight to look around the area so that he would remember where the money was located. When his flashlight shined on his watch for a second, Jupiter saw the time. His eyes bulged out of his sockets.

"Oh, no, Penny!" He ran back the way he had come and went back up the sewer manhole. Jupiter then retraced all his steps back to school.

When Jupiter got to the school to pick up Penny, she was nowhere to be found. He searched around the school and then went inside. He saw Penny's second grade teacher and ran to her.

"Have you seen my sister, Penelope?" he asked praying that she had. He was breathing heavily.

"Yeah, she left school about thirty minutes ago."

"With who?" Jupiter was surprised.

"Her Uncle Tony. Your Aunt Justine put him on the list."

Without saying another word, Jupiter bolted out of the school. He feared the worst would happen to Penny being alone with Uncle Tony.

About an hour later, Jupiter made it home. Everyone in the house was eating dinner at the table. His eyes quickly scanned for Penny. He smiled when he saw her. His uncle Tony came over to him. They went into Uncle Tony's room on the first floor.

"What took you so long?" Uncle Tony asked looking at him suspiciously. "Don't get like your momma."

Uncle Tony's son, Jabari, came to the doorway and looked on. He anticipated Jupiter getting in trouble with his father. He wanted to see Jupiter hurt again.

Jupiter didn't understand Uncle Tony's reference. He handed Barry's backpack to him.

"Is it all here?" Uncle Tony slit his eyes at him.

"I don't know. I didn't look in the bag."

Uncle Tony looked in the bag and saw stacks of money. "You might get a bonus from this." He chuckled as he glanced over at Jabari. "Good work. So what did you have to do to get this?"

"Pop, you better make sure he didn't steal some of the money." Jabari frowned. "I don't trust him."

Uncle Tony ignored his son's comment. "What did you say?" he asked Jupiter again.

"Nothing. I just asked, and he gave." Jupiter tried to be cool and calm.

"Good answer. We don't need any snitches around here. Go eat. Hold up."

"Yeah," Jupiter said nervously.

"What happened to your backpack?"

Jupiter smiled at him. "I got some ketchup on it and threw it away."

Uncle Tony winked at him. "Ketchup. I'll get you another one tonight."

Jabari stormed away from the door.

"Thanks, Uncle Tony," Jupiter said as he left the room and went to eat.

After he left the room, Uncle Tony counted the money on his bed. Uncle Tony couldn't help but think about what Jupiter had done to Barry to get this money back for him. Though he laughed, Uncle Tony did see a dangerous side to his nephew that he wanted to use.

❧

The next day couldn't have come fast enough for Jupiter. He and Penny ate breakfast like every other day, but Jupiter seemed happier than normal. As they left the house and headed down to the bus stop, they saw Jabari drive pass them in his new red Ford Mustang. After seeing him, he and Penny stopped in the middle of the block.

"Penny, I'm going to pick you up early today," he said looking into his sister's eyes.

"Where are we going?" she asked out of curiosity.

Jupiter smiled. "Somewhere special."

Her eyes lit up out of excitement. "Are we going to the park? Please, please, say park. I love the park."

"Nope, not the park. It's a surprise, but just in case, we don't go today, don't tell anybody and that includes Auntie and Uncle Tony."

"Okay."

"It's going to be great," he said as they finished their walk to the bus stop.

∽

That afternoon at school, Jupiter faked being sick and got excused to go home. He left the school still feeling great as he crossed the school yard. He went back to the alley manhole and went down it. This time, Jupiter had brought a big flashlight. He walked down to where he hid his backpack with the money and dug it up. He opened the bag and touched the money. It made him feel liberated.

"Let's go get Penny," he said to himself as he got up and left.

∽

As Jupiter and Penny crossed the street by the school, he noticed Uncle Tony's car pulling up in front. He exhaled with joy knowing he had missed him. Penny saw Uncle Tony's car as well.

"Let's get a ride with Uncle Tony."

"No." Jupiter quickly led her down the street and onto the city bus that pulled up.

"Where are we going?" Penny asked.

"Penny, this is the surprise that I was talking about. We're taking a trip." Jupiter smiled at her hoping that she would be happy.

"Really!" she said getting happier. "What time will we be back?"

They sat down on the back of the bus. "Penny, we're not ever coming back," he said. He knew Penny was still too young to quite understand what Auntie and Uncle Tony did for a living. Plus, he didn't want to go into the whole Uncle Tony being a pedophile story.

Penny sat there thinking about what her brother had just said. She didn't want to go, but she saw the pain in his face. Though he thought she was too young to understand, Penny actually knew that it wasn't easy for him. "Okay Jupiter, whatever you say."

He reached out and hugged her. "Thank you."

"Where are we going?" she asked again.

"California. Oakland, California," he said.

"Why there?" she asked. "How are we getting there?"

"We're catching the bus. I'm going to see my father."

"Your father?" she was stunned. "You know him? How? You have a father?"

He paused to think about her 'you know him' question. "No, I don't know him, but I don't know if he knows about me. I found his name in momma's notebook and looked him up on the internet at school."

"Is he picking us up?"

"No, that's why we're catching the bus."

"I'm hungry," Penny said changing the subject. "Can I eat first?"

"I'll get us plenty of food before we get on the bus. It's going to be a long trip. Don't worry, I'll take care of us."

She smiled at him. "No school tomorrow. Yea."

Jupiter smiled. It made him feel at ease that she seemed comfortable with his decision to travel cross country to see his father. In the back of his mind, he couldn't shake thoughts of how his father might welcome him into his life. But in his mind, he felt that this was the better alternative than staying with his aunt and uncle.

At the school, Uncle Tony was talking to Penny's teacher. The teacher had just told him that Jupiter picked her up about fifteen minutes prior. He went back outside and looked around the school yard. He wondered what Jupiter was up too. After about five minutes later, he gave up and left.

CHAPTER NINE

I t took three days before they finally made it to California. The bus ride to Oakland was an adventure that they would cherish forever. They had a strong bond already, but now it was even stronger. Throughout the entire trip, they lived it up to the fullest. Jupiter made sure they were fed and that whatever Penny wanted, she got. He made sure to never cause a stir or start a lot of conversations. The last thing he wanted was to discuss his age or why he and his sister were going to California. For the trip, he spent about fifteen hundred dollars out of the thirty thousand. As they stepped out of the bus, they were tired and looking for an actual bed to sleep on.

Once her feet hit the California pavement, Penny turned to him. "Where to now?" she asked.

Jupiter looked at her and then down at his pre-paid phone that he bought at the Walgreens by the bus station in Memphis. He saw a cab and began waving it down. "We're heading to the train station," he said to Penny.

"What about your father?" she asked excited.

"We'll hopefully see him tomorrow. I want us to be rested and looking good."

The cab stopped and they got in.

"Take us to Fruitvale Station please," Jupiter said to the cab driver.

When they got to Fruitvale Station, Jupiter quickly took Penny into the men's restroom and locked the door.

"What are we doing in here?" she asked.

"We're going to stay here for tonight only." Jupiter looked at her sadly hoping she would understand.

"Can't we just go to your dad's place? I'm tired."

Jupiter sighed. "Penny, we have to stay here until tomorrow. Just do this for me, please."

"This doesn't seem right."

"I saw Will Smith stay here in a movie. He and his son made it through the night. We can too."

Someone knocked on the door. Jupiter put his finger over his mouth to indicate that Penny should be quiet as well. The person stopped knocking and walked away.

"Just until the morning and then we will go see my father. Everything will be okay after that. I promise." Jupiter wasn't sure about the promise he had just made, but hoped that he was telling the truth. He needed something good to happen in their life because he didn't want to ever return back to Memphis.

❧

The next morning, Jupiter woke up with a nervous anticipation. He couldn't wait to see the man who was his father. He didn't know how he would address him or bring up the 'I think you're my dad' situation. He woke up Penny, laying next to him on top of some newspapers, trying to mask his nervousness.

"We have to get ready to go," he said. "We need to hit the mall and then go to my father's house."

Penny sat up. "I'm tired Jupiter. Can I sleep longer?"

"You can sleep tonight in a real place."

"Are we staying at your dad's?"

Jupiter thought briefly about it. "No, I don't want to do that. We don't know him."

"But he's your dad," Penny said. "Doesn't he want us to stay with him?"

"Just hurry up. We need to look nice." He was happy as could be but held it in. Knowing that he actually had a father was a big deal for him. He always wanted a good father figure and felt that if his father knew he existed, that he would embrace him with outpouring love and affection.

Jupiter went to the sink and starting washing his face and body.

❧

Over at Justine's home office in the basement, she and Uncle Tony sat wondering where the hell Jupiter and Penny might have gone. It had been four days since they disappeared. Up until now, they had told the school and anyone outside of the house that Jupiter and Penny were recovering from chicken pox. With it now being at the four day mark, Justine knew the chicken pox story wouldn't work much longer if they couldn't produce the kids. She didn't say anything, but deep down she began to think that Uncle Tony had done something to them and didn't want to tell her.

"So, you don't have any idea of where they are?" she asked looking him straight in the face. "If we don't find them soon, that will be a big issue for us."

"What are you talking about? I didn't touch them at all." Uncle Tony got defensive. "I can't believe you're trying to put this on me. It's that boy. He's just like his momma, just trouble."

"Growing up, you use to think Maggie was the world. Now you hate her and her kids." Justine said slitting her eyes at him. "Maggie is still blood. Her kids are family."

63

"Times change. She wasn't right stealing from us."

"She stole from me. I love her. She will always be my sister. I just want Clyde dead and my money back."

"So she gets off clean?" Uncle Tony said.

Justine sat up in her chair. "What do you want? To kill her? This is Maggie we're talking about. Are you crazy?" Justine rolled her eyes at him. "You want to kill your sister?"

"I'm just saying."

"Saying nothing. Let's focus on these kids. The school is going to report them not coming to school four days in a row and then it'll hit the police. We don't have a doctor's note. I can't have the police and the news over here on some citywide manhunt for these kids. That's bad for business. We got to find them. What about Barry? Do you think he could have done something to them?" Justine asked.

Uncle Tony shook his head for no. "Barry couldn't hurt a fly right now. Jupiter burnt him up pretty bad. I went back to their old neighborhood and had the boys looking for them as well. Ain't nobody seen them at all. It's like they disappeared into thin air or something."

"Jupiter's a smart kid. He's somewhere. I just got to think where he might be. They don't have any money, food, or other family."

"Maybe his father got him?" Uncle Tony laughed out loud.

"That's one thing we don't have to worry about. I still can't believe my sister doesn't know her kids father. That and her choice of Clyde for a man will always puzzle me." Justine mustered up a regrettable grin.

"So what do you want to do?"

Justine sat there running different scenarios in her head to avoid unwanted attention and then it hit her. "Tell all the kids that they are not to work for the next couple of days, have a cleaning service come in now, and pick up that one thousand keys that Julius has for us at the docks."

"No problem sis. It's done. I'll have the boys moving that weight tonight."

"No, not for a few days. Put it over at the storage unit."

"Anything else?" he asked.

"Hit me!" she said bracing herself to be hit.

Uncle Tony didn't quite know what she meant. "What are you saying?"

"Hit me across the face. I need to convince the police that Jupiter was out of control. He beat me up and kidnapped his sister. If he's looked at as being violent then there will be less attention on finding him, and we can continue our business with minimal interruption. Nobody cares about two black kids, especially if it's a juvenile delinquent running away with his sister after he beat up his charitable, loving aunt. That will keep people out on the street looking for them and not at our house."

Uncle Tony stood up. "Are you sure?"

"This has to happen. Tomorrow, we'll call the police and explain to them Jupiter's violent behavior. Hit me. These bruises have to look fresh, but old."

"You sure you don't want to wait another day. If they don't turn up, maybe they're dead."

"Do you know something that you're not telling me?" Justine slit her eyes at him.

"I didn't touch those kids. And I don't know where they are at. Stop assuming the worst, Justine."

"Just hit me."

"Just for the record, I think we should give it one more day. Here it comes."

She nodded. He then hit her across the face with his fist. Justine touched her face.

"You hit like a girl. Hit me again," she said as he struck again. Justine touched her face and then saw blood on her hand. She tasted it. "That's what I'm talking about."

❧

Later that same day, Jupiter and Penny's cab pulled up in the Oakland Hills at a home that was surrounded by a security gate. The home was huge and took up about twenty-five thousand square feet. From outside, the three story home looked relatively new. When the cab stopped, Jupiter looked at the address he had again. The cab driver saw him as well. He didn't think the siblings belonged in this neighborhood.

"Kid, are you sure this is where you're going?" The cab driver asked looking at them both.

Penny shrugged her shoulders as she looked at her brother.

"Yeah, this is my father's house," Jupiter said with a smile.

"Does he know you're coming? Looks kind of empty," the cabbie said sarcastically.

Jupiter rolled his eyes. "How much?" he asked.

The cab driver looked at his meter. "That's forty dollars."

Jupiter handed him forty dollars. He and Penny got out of the cab.

"You want me to wait?" the cab driver asked.

Jupiter looked at the house again. He smiled. "No, we'll be okay. Thanks."

The cab driver took off, and Jupiter and Penny walked over to the intercom system outside the gate.

"Your daddy has a big house," Penny said excited for Jupiter. "He must be rich."

Jupiter didn't respond. His eyes were fixated on the intercom button. He didn't know what he was going to say when asked who he was. He looked around the property then pressed the button.

"Hello, may I help you, young man?" a man's voice said through the intercom.

Jupiter scanned around to see where a camera might be. He didn't see one.

"Why are you here?" the man asked.

Jupiter cleared the lump in his throat. "I'm here to see a Marcellus Jupiter Carpenter."

"Do I know you?" the man asked curiously. "Who told you my middle name?"

"My name is Jupiter Jones, sir."

There was silence for about a minute then the gate opened. From the gate, Jupiter and Penny saw the front door of the house open. They went inside the gate and headed toward the door. Marcellus came out and stood in the doorway. Jupiter saw the resemblance and by Marcellus's agonized look, he did too.

"Why did you come here?" Marcellus asked as they approached his door.

"I think you're my father," Jupiter said staring at Marcellus in wonderment. He saw that they had the same eyes, nose, and head shape.

"I think you have the wrong guy," Marcellus said shockingly. It was a lie that he and Jupiter knew he was telling.

"You don't know a Maggie Jones from Memphis, Tennessee?"

Marcellus played dumb. "Never heard of her. Is she famous?"

Jupiter didn't know what to say. He was at a loss. By how much he resembled Marcellus, it seemed impossible for them to not be related.

"Are you Jupiter's father?" Penny asked.

Marcellus looked at both of them and said with a straight face. "No. I'm sorry young man, but someone has terribly misinformed you. I'm not your father or yours either, little girl. Sorry."

Jupiter was befuddled. "Have you ever lived in Memphis?"

"No," Marcellus said lying once more. He nervously cleared his throat. "Is your mother near here?"

Jupiter was dejected. "No, she left us. I saw your name in her diary. I just thought you were my father," he said as he started crying. "All my research pointed to you."

"Where do you kids live now?"

"Memphis," Jupiter replied.

"How did you get out here?" Marcellus asked.

"We caught the bus. I'm sorry for disturbing you. I never had a father growing up. I just wanted to meet him once in my lifetime."

Marcellus checked his watch anxiously. It was obvious he needed them to leave soon. "I can take you somewhere if you like. Where are you staying?" Marcellus glanced behind them. "No grownups came with you?"

"No, we left because of our aunt and uncle. They aren't good people. They are drug dealers," Jupiter said hoping to gain some sympathy. "They have me selling drugs for them. We need help."

Marcellus cared nothing about their aunt or uncle being drug dealers or about them making him sell drugs. Jupiter's words fell on deaf ears. "I can buy you a plane ticket to get back to Memphis. When are you leaving?"

Jupiter shook his head like it didn't matter anymore. "I don't know. I guess we can leave tomorrow."

Marcellus checked his pockets for his car keys and slowly closed the front door. "Let's get in the car over there quickly. I'll take you to where you're staying and get you a couple of plane tickets. Where are you staying?"

"We stayed in a public restroom last night," Jupiter said fuming at him.

"I'll get you two a room for the night and then you can go from there to the airport."

"You look so much like my brother," Penny said smiling at Marcellus. "You sure you're not my brother's father?"

"They say I look like a lot of people. Get in the car." Marcellus opened up the car door and shoved them inside. "Make sure you don't get my seats dirty."

"Okay," Jupiter said, staring at him wishing he would tell the truth.

Marcellus took off fast from his driveway. While he was going out of his gate, a black woman with two twin girls, around Penny's age, was arriving. The girls resembled Jupiter.

It had been about two hours, but Marcellus did everything that he said he would do. He got them plane tickets and got them a hotel room. Though Marcellus had said that he wasn't his father, Jupiter knew that wasn't the truth. He wanted to say something to Marcellus at the time, but saw no reason to try to convince him of something he knew himself. He just couldn't bring himself to tell Penny how low down and disrespectful his father had just treated him. His face told that story. Jupiter looked like a broken kid.

"Are we going back home tomorrow, Jupiter?" Penny asked as they walked back in their hotel room.

Jupiter nodded his head and went to the bathroom. Once inside, he turned on the water and cried sitting on the floor. His heart was ripped into pieces and his soul destroyed. He had no clue how to repair his broken spirit. Going back to Memphis wasn't part of his escape plan. With it now being the only option, Jupiter racked his brain trying to figure out what to say to his aunt and uncle once they returned.

When he emerged from the bathroom, he went over and sat down next to Penny. When we get back tomorrow, I need you to help me."

"Do what?"

"If you tell anybody that we came to California, something real bad will happen to me. They will probably split us up."

"No, Jupiter, no." Penny pouted. "They can't do that."

"They can, but that's why I need for you to tell the same story that I tell everyone. Can you do that Penny?" Jupiter hated having her lie, but that was the only way any story could work.

"Okay. What do I say?" she asked nervously. Penny knew that it was going to be hard for her to lie.

"I'm going to have to hurt myself, and we are going to go to the hospital once we land tomorrow."

"Hurt yourself?" Penny's eyes grew.

"If there was another way, I would take it." Jupiter was convinced that no other options existed.

"What about Auntie and Uncle Tony?"

"We will have the hospital call them and say where we are at. When they get there, we will tell them that three white guys grabbed us and said that our mother owed them money. They broke my arm and said that was just a message. Can you handle that?" he asked Penny trying to gauge her comprehension of his plan. "Then we'll say we escaped."

Penny stared at him like he was out of his mind. "You're going to break your arm?"

"I have to. No one can know about our trip or the money. I need you on my team, okay?"

"I'll practice it and get it right," Penny said proudly.

⤱

Jupiter and Penny landed back in Memphis. It still hurt that his father didn't claim him, but he moved on for now because he had bigger problems to deal with. Following the story that he told Penny, they went to the hospital and outside in the parking lot he broke his left arm against a light pole. The pain was excruciating for him, personally, and mentally for Penny, who had to watch. They then ran to the emergency room where Jupiter told the security guard their story.

The emergency room took him in immediately and put his arm in a cast. They also called Justine to tell her what happened. Justine and Uncle Tony were there waiting when he and Penny got back from the casting area. The police were there too, but Justine told them she needed to speak with her niece and nephew first, so they waited down the hallway.

"Hey, Auntie and Uncle Tony," Jupiter said with sorrow in his voice. He made his pain look real.

"What happened?" Justine asked.

"Three white guys grabbed us the other day after I picked Penny up from school. They took us somewhere and threatened us. Something about Mom owing them a lot of money. They scared us."

"What did they want?" Uncle Tony asked, but didn't really buy the story.

"They said my mother owed them a cut from a bank job. I was just worried about Penny and I being safe. They had a lot of guns. I think they talked to Mom."

"Why they let you go?" Justine asked, doubting his story as well.

"They didn't. After they broke my arm, I grabbed Penny and we got out of there. I wish I could have called you." Jupiter reached out and hugged his aunt.

Justine turned her attention to Penny. She knew if the story was fake, Penny would be the one to prove it. "So Penny, how are you? Did the two white men scare you?"

"There were three men, Auntie," Penny said correcting her. "I thought they were going to kill Jupiter. I'm so glad to be back."

Justine began to believe the story. "When did you escape?"

Jupiter's stomach fell to the floor, hearing that question. He hadn't rehearsed that question with her.

"Today, before we got to the hospital." Penny frowned. "Jupiter doesn't feel well. Look what they did to my brother."

Justine looked over at Uncle Tony. They didn't know what to say. On one end, they thought he was lying, but on the other end, he did have Penny in sync with his story. The broken arm was the main selling point for them that made his story seem plausible. And though they knew Jupiter was smart, they didn't think he would go to the extent of breaking his own arm.

"Uncle Tony, go take care of the bill. We'll meet you out front." Justine looked over at Jupiter. "Are you ready to head back home?"

"I missed it so much," Jupiter said reaching out to be hugged by his aunt. She did oblige. He and Uncle Tony stared at each other with no emotion. "I love you, Auntie."

Justine smiled. "That's what I like to hear. You're leadership material. Take one for the team type of guy. You don't find people like that anymore." Justine looked at Uncle Tony. "Tell the officers we will handle it ourselves. Didn't I tell you to go pay the bill? I want to get out of here now."

Uncle Tony left the room.

Just hearing her make demands of the officers made Jupiter's skin crawl. He knew that she had connections high up. He was now seeing how widespread it was. His eyes welled up, knowing that it would almost be impossible to escape his aunt's world again. The meeting with his dad crossed his mind. The pain of the denial came back. Jupiter cried. His aunt thought it was his arm. She comforted him.

"You're home now," she said touching his good arm. "This will never happen to you again. You're my family. I will kill for you and Penny."

"What happened to you?" he asked looking at the bruises on her face.

Justine smiled. "Just being foolish."

CHAPTER TEN

I t had been about six months since the Barry incident and cross country trek to Oakland. The broken arm and the story of the white guys kidnapping them gave Jupiter and Penny huge sympathy points. It was a big part of why the past six months had been great for them. They were doing excellent in school, and their home life was going well. Even their aunt and uncle seemed to have put what their mother had done to them in the past. They were starting to fit in with the other foster kids at the house. They did open their eyes and take notice that the other foster kids were rarely at the house outside of leaving in the morning for school and dinner, but that was just to eat and then they left again. The kids usually wouldn't return until midnight. The time they did all spend together was mainly Saturday and Sunday morning and afternoons until the kids disappeared again until the wee hours of the morning.

On this Saturday evening, Jupiter and Penny were in the living room as the other kids were getting ready to leave. Normally, Jupiter didn't ask questions that he didn't want to know the answers to, but today he felt curious and a little bored.

"Hey Gideon, where you going?" Jupiter asked.

Gideon was one of the older foster kids. He was eighteen years old and had been with Justine since he was eight. He was kind of the leader who made sure all the other kids stayed in line, except for Jupiter and Penny, since they were blood relatives of Justine. They lived by separate rules. Outside of the Barry job, Jupiter didn't have to do anything else for the business, but the lives of the other foster kids wasn't so clean. They ran drugs for Justine all over the city, in the school, in the park, and on the street corners. Her operation was vast and the biggest drug ring in the state.

Gideon looked around to make sure no adults were listening. "You're joking right?"

"No, I don't know." Jupiter shrugged his shoulders. Gideon stared at him for a second thinking about what he should really say. "Nothing is free around here, Jup. You might want to take off them blinders."

A dark shadow overcame Jupiter, he remembered Uncle Tony saying the same thing to him. He couldn't imagine the magnitude of what Gideon and the others had to endure. Though he was just fifteen years old now, he still understood that Gideon's hope for a better life was already lost.

"Do you want me to go with you?" Jupiter asked.

"That might not be a good idea," Gideon said shaking his head. "Your uncle is a trip. You know your cousin is a snitch ass."

"I won't tell, if you don't tell. I just want to see what goes on at night. Nobody cares about what Jabari thinks."

"I know this is probably going to be a big mistake. If I take you, you better listen to me every time. If I say run, we run, okay?"

"Can I go?" Penny asked.

Jupiter smiled at her. "No Penny. I'm going to go out with Gideon. Just for tonight, okay?"

Penny gave him a sad face. "We always spend Saturdays together watching TV."

He gave her a hug. "I know. I'm sorry. Auntie will be home with you."

"I don't want to spend time with Auntie," she said pouting.

"I'll make it up to you, I promise, next week."

"Hey, Jup, we all gotta go. You in?" Gideon asked as he walked toward the door to join the others.

Jupiter looked at Penny again. She nodded for him to go. "I'm coming."

He kissed Penny on the cheek and left with Gideon and the others. From the third floor window, Jabari looked down on them walking away from the house.

❧

That night, Jupiter was introduced to the world of drug dealing from the bottom of the totem pole. The corners where Gideon took him were where they earned their stripes on the streets. Located not far from downtown, the streets were packed with customers wanting a fix. Though he had been just watching the entire night, Jupiter wanted to get the feel of what it was like selling drugs on the corner. From his experience with dropping off the package to Barry, he had a little insight, but this was real selling. The danger intrigued him.

As Jupiter stood next to Gideon waiting on the next customer to roll by, he nudged Gideon on the arm.

"Can I do the next one?" Jupiter asked.

Gideon slit his eyes at him. He wasn't sure that Jupiter was up for the task. "Maybe another time."

"I can handle it. I just want see how it feels."

"Jup, you do know this isn't a game. This is real life out here. Things can go wrong quickly. I don't want anything to happen to you. Justine wouldn't let that slide."

"She wouldn't do anything to you."

Gideon shook his head at his naivity. "You're blood. You're like a made man in the mob. I'm not. I'm expendable trash."

"You're not trash. You're my friend."

Gideon took a deep breath. "Okay, just once."

Jupiter smiled. "Cool. Thanks man."

The next customer pulled up. Jupiter slowly walked over to his car. He leaned into the driver side window.

"What's going on tonight?" he asked the person driving.

"I need something good," the person said as they handed him a roll of money. "The good stuff."

"Be right back," Jupiter said as he walked back over to Gideon. He gave Gideon the money. Gideon went around the back of the store and then came back around. He gave Jupiter a package. Jupiter ran back over to the car and handed it to the person.

"Have a good night," he said as the driver sped off down the street.

Jupiter went back to where Gideon stood as another car pulled up. Gideon started to walk to the car, but Jupiter stopped him.

"Last one, this is fun."

"Go ahead," Gideon said shaking his head. He couldn't believe Jupiter referenced selling drugs on the street corner on a Saturday night as fun.

Jupiter, with his dark hoodie covering his face, went over to the car.

"It's a great night outside tonight. What do you think about the night?" he asked the older balding white man sitting behind the wheel. One look at the man and Jupiter froze. He couldn't believe that his school principal was in the car. He wanted to say something to him, but no words came out.

"Terrible. Why do you think I'm out here?" his principal asked. Then he thought about the voice of the kid. "Do I know you?"

Jupiter changed his voice to be much deeper. "What do you want? I don't have all night."

His principal handed him two thousand dollars. "That should cover me for the weekend. Only the best. Tell Gideon its P.W."

Jupiter took the money and ran it over to Gideon.

"Hey Gideon, I think I'm just going to head back home."

Gideon looked at him, surprised. His glowing mood from drug dealing being fun seemed to have died quickly. "Is everything alright?"

Jupiter looked back at the car. "I just need to go check on Penny. I'm sorry man. The guy in the car said his name was P.W."

"Oh snap. Cool. Go ahead. I'll see you later." Gideon went behind the store again to get the drugs while Jupiter walked off down the street.

Jupiter got home a little before midnight. As he entered from the door, he saw a little girl about twelve run by him crying heading out the door. Uncle Tony came out the room half dressed.

"Where you been?" he asked Jupiter.

"I was doing some homework with some classmates."

"What you saw you didn't see, right?" Uncle Tony stared down at him.

Jupiter thought what he had been doing was plain disgusting. He wanted Uncle Tony to burn for what he was doing to these little girls.

"Are you okay, Uncle Tony?" Jupiter asked staring at him.

Uncle Tony threw him up against the wall. "What you mean, am I okay?"

"Nothing." Jupiter threw his hands up in the air.

"That's what I thought. You don't want to see Penny in there. I like them around that age," Uncle Tony whispered in his ear.

Jupiter snatched away from him. "Stay away from Penny."

"Are you going to be trouble?" Uncle Tony asked as he threw Jupiter back up against the wall. "I don't want to hurt you. And I know you don't want to leave Penny here alone." He smiled.

Jupiter wanted to kill him, but having no weapon and with his uncle having a significant size advantage over him , it was a wish that would have to wait until another day.

"You be a good boy and go to your room. And next time I hear about you on one of my corners, Gideon will be dead. You're a Jones, we don't do the corners."

"Gideon didn't have anything to do with it." Jupiter figured Jabari had snitched on him. "I went on my own."

"He knows the rules."

"Don't do anything to him. It was my fault," Jupiter said.

"Get your little ass up them stairs now! And don't say another damn word."

Jupiter held in what he wanted to say and stomped up the stairs. He felt bad that he had gotten Gideon in trouble over his desire to go to the corners. By the look on Uncle Tony's face, he knew Gideon wouldn't be given a break for taking him without authorization.

◈

When Jupiter and Penny came down for breakfast the next morning, none of the other kids were there. At the table were just Uncle Tony and Jabari, who both looked angry.

"Good morning," Uncle Tony said. Jabari rolled his eyes and didn't say a word.

"Good morning, Uncle Tony," they both said at the same time.

"Where everybody at?" Jupiter asked.

"This is what happens when the leader of a group doesn't lead by example. He brings everyone else down with him. We have very simple rules around here. Listen to me and Justine, and your life will be fine. Don't, and you might as well call the coroner yourself."

"Are they coming back?"

"Do they teach you anything in school? What I look like firing all my labor? People here work for life. Of course they'll be back. When you're done eating, I need you to go to the store for me."

"Okay, Penny and I will go right after breakfast."

"Penny stays here," Uncle Tony said with a growl.

"Why?" Jupiter asked getting mad at the sight of his uncle.

"Don't question my pops, fool!" Jabari smirked. "I hate this buster."

"I never have to explain myself to you. Eat and come to my room when you're done so I can tell you what to get." Uncle Tony got up and walked off.

"I can't go," Penny said with sadness in her voice.

"No, you need to stay here," Jupiter said with just as much sadness himself. He sat down and stared at his breakfast. With the new turn of events, he was no longer hungry.

Penny sat down and started eating immediately. She saw Jupiter just staring and stopped eating herself.

Jabari smiled at Jupiter then got up from the table. He headed out of the front door and left in his car.

"What's wrong Jupiter? Is there anything I can do?" Penny asked.

Jupiter cracked a small smile and swiped his eyes removing the tears that had formed. "I'll figure it out. I'll run to Uncle Tony now and head to the store. I'll be back soon."

"Okay."

Jupiter got close in her face and whispered. "Like I told you before, I need for you to stay away from Uncle Tony. Can you do that?"

"Yes, okay," Penny replied. "But he seems like such a nice person."

Jupiter walked off and went to Uncle Tony's room. He noticed that his door was slightly opened. Jupiter slowly went inside. When he got inside the room, he saw Beverly, one of the foster kids, sleeping in Uncle Tony's bed. She was his age. As he stood there thinking about how sick his Uncle was, he knew he had to stop him before he went after Penny.

From behind, Uncle Tony grabbed his shoulder. "Who told you to come in my damn room?"

Jupiter jumped. He grabbed his chest. "I was just coming to find out what you needed me to get from the store."

Uncle Tony reached on his dresser and passed a note to him. "Here. You should be able to read the writing."

Jupiter looked at the note. Seeing that it was a grocery list, he was a little perturbed that he needed him to make that run, but as always, he knew he was in no position to say no.

"I can read it."

Uncle Tony handed him some money. "That should cover it. Tell Larry I said take you."

"Okay," Jupiter said glancing over at Beverly sleeping. He also saw a knife on the dresser. His first thought was to grab it and stab Uncle Tony. Jupiter was afraid of what the consequences might be if he missed. So, he just stood there.

Uncle Tony saw him looking toward the knife. "Get!" He pushed Jupiter out the door. "You're not man enough to kill me."

As Jupiter was walking out, he grabbed Penny and brought her with him. He knew there would be deep repercussions when he got back, but it was better than leaving her at the house alone with Uncle Tony.

⌘

That evening when Jupiter came back with Penny and the groceries, he saw a badly beaten Gideon sitting down watching TV. He went to talk to him.

"Hey Gideon, I'm so sorry, man. I didn't mean for that to happen to you. It's my entire fault."

Gideon looked at him and then saw Uncle Tony come up behind Jupiter. "It was all my fault man. I knew better."

"It wasn't on you." Jupiter turned around and saw Uncle Tony. "Hey, Uncle Tony."

Uncle Tony gave him a devilish grin. "I could have sworn that I told you to go by yourself and to leave Penny here. Was I not clear?"

"I thought you were joking," Jupiter said with a smile. His smile was not reciprocated by his uncle.

"You must think I'm a joke."

Jupiter saw the anger in his eyes. "No, I don't think that. I'm sorry if I got confused."

"You will be sorry today." Uncle Tony looked at all the other kids in the room. "If your name is not Jupiter, you better go to your room now."

The other kids scampered. Penny was the only one to stay.

"Penny, you better leave right now," Uncle Tony said to her raising his voice.

She looked over at Jupiter.

"Go Penny. I'll be okay," Jupiter said trying to reassure her that things would be alright.

"You'll be okay, huh?" Uncle Tony chuckled. "Brave heart! I wish Jabari was here. I'd have him kick your ass all over this house."

Jupiter stared at him. "I'd like to see him try."

Penny left but kept looking back to check on her brother as she went upstairs to their room.

With everyone gone, Uncle Tony and Jupiter stood face to face. Jupiter was a little bit scared just thinking about what he might do to him. He did find comfort that he had saved his sister from Uncle Tony.

Suddenly, Uncle Tony hit Jupiter in the nose. Blood splattered everywhere. Jupiter fell to the ground. His uncle jumped on him and punched him everywhere he could. Then out of the clear blue, someone hit Uncle Tony across the head with a walking cane. Uncle Tony turned around with vengeance. He was ready to rip the person's head off for hitting him. When he saw that it was his sister, Justine, he ceased any attempts at retribution.

"Have you lost your mind?" Justine asked with her walking cane cocked back. She was ready to hit him again if necessary.

"The boy needs to be taught a lesson," Uncle Tony said as if pouting. "He doesn't listen."

"And you do? I told you to not touch him. He's family."

"But..."

"But nothing! Get him up and clean him up. I hope you can get that blood out of my carpet." Justine shook her head. "You want me to go to jail for abusing a child. These are my foster kids. If he goes to school and his teacher reports this, we'll start having eyes on us. That's the kind of attention that I don't need for my business. Look at what you did to Gideon. Why don't you beat that dumb ass kid you got? He keeps stealing shit around here like I don't know it. Control him first and leave these kids to me."

"I'm sorry." Uncle Tony reluctantly helped Jupiter off the ground and gave him a tissue.

"Are you okay Jupiter?" Justine asked him. "You're the future of this family. I'll see to that. This won't happen again. You have my promise. Ain't that right Uncle Tony?"

"It won't happen again," Uncle Tony said frowning.

Though he was saved this time, he knew that Uncle Tony would now try to hurt him in other ways. It was at that moment that Jupiter knew he would have to kill his uncle Tony in order to ever have peace within the household.

Justine placed her hand on Jupiter's shoulder. "It's about time you get more acquainted with our operation. This is just a small part of what we do."

Jupiter looked her in the eyes. "I guess I can't say no."

"That's not an option here," Justine said. "Are we clear?"

Jupiter took a deep breath. He knew this was the beginning of the end for him. Though he wasn't the low man on the totem pole, he knew the life he had planned for himself was about to be seriously altered.

"Very clear Auntie."

CHAPTER ELEVEN

A s promised, Justine started Jupiter on the road to being the next drug kingpin in the family. Though against his will, Jupiter knew he had no choice in the matter. Being fifteen and a half, he knew that he needed a better plan than the last one. His ill-advised plan stayed on his mind right along with thoughts of killing his biological father. He knew his next plan had to be strategized completely and needed to be well-funded. A major part of his plan was to bide his time and skim off the top of the money coming in. He hated his current life. Justine had him overseeing the movement of drugs in his high school and the other high schools in Memphis. He also managed the work of the other foster kids working the streets late night.

At school, Jupiter kept his underworld ties quiet. Drugs moved through the school, but very few knew who was actually behind it. Most of Jupiter's captains were the popular kids who loved the money and the attention. They operated under a strict code of silence; if they told on Jupiter, they or a family member would be seriously hurt. He knew his connections scared those captains and dealers.

On the streets, he was now Gideon's boss. Knowing the stakes were too high to repeat the mistakes of his last plan to leave, he followed Justine and Uncle Tony's instructions to a fault. If someone needed to be taught a lesson, he made sure they learned it. Jupiter had become a real leader in Justine's drug network within a matter of a few months. Even Uncle Tony took notice and began to get more jealous.

It was lunch time in the cafeteria and as usual, Jupiter sat with his best friend, Miguel. Miguel was a Black Puerto Rican who talked fast but was almost as smart as Jupiter. Miguel, though, was from a stable home in the suburbs with two parents, two siblings, and two dogs. He was Jupiter's friend and admired his street cred. Seeing the way people treated Jupiter and hearing the stories made Miguel envious of his lifestyle. But outside of Gideon and Penny, Miguel had earned Jupiter's trust. He told him things that now endangered Miguel's life.

"Did you see Angela today? She asked about you during second period," Miguel said with a smirk. "She's always asking about you. You need to hit that."

Jupiter raised his head up from his food tray. He stopped eating. Jupiter hadn't paid Miguel much attention until now. "What she want to know?"

"Just basic stuff."

"What you tell her? You better not tell her about me," Jupiter said shaking his head.

"She's in to you like crazy. Girl was writing poems about you in class. She's a bad ass. I would love to hit that."

"Really." Jupiter was surprised that she felt that way about him. "She never acts like she likes me. Chick doesn't even speak."

"Look around, Jup. People are afraid of you," Miguel said nodding his head. "And it's not like you make it any better. You don't talk to nobody. You go to class and only hang out with me. Nobody ever bothers you."

"Consider yourself lucky." Jupiter smiled. "I don't have time for any of this."

"My pops always tells me that you have to make time for yourself. At least that's what he tells my mom when he comes home late at night."

Jupiter hated hearing about Miguel's father's advice. It only added fire to his personal struggles of life. But he knew Miguel and his father had a good relationship, so he acted as if he cared.

"You have a cool dad."

"We went to the Grizzlies game the other night and sat in the front row. I thought about tripping a referee for fun. I met all the players."

"Yeah, it's too bad he didn't come through with that ticket for me," Jupiter said lowering his head.

Miguel saw the dejection but didn't want to address it head on. "Maybe next time."

He rose up and stared at Miguel. "Next time? I doubt that man. Your father is not going to bring me to any game with you two."

"Why not?" Miguel asked confused.

"Man, you cannot be that naïve to think that your uncle, the assistant general manager of the Grizzlies, can't get an extra ticket to a game." Jupiter shook his head again. "That's your father's brother. One more ticket shouldn't be a big deal."

"That's not true. He's not like that." Miguel tried to defend his father but realized that there was truth in Jupiter's words.

"It's the reality of life. The haves versus the have nots."

Miguel laughed. "You act like I'm royalty or something."

"Still something higher than where I come from. I'm from the dirt and trying to crawl out of a grave. I'm a slave of the universe."

"You have the same chances I do."

Jupiter was about to say more then stopped. He figured that it was a waste of time explaining the difference between his life as a foster child running drugs for his aunt and Miguel's life where his father worked for the government and his mother was a pediatric doctor.

"I got to check some traps real quick before class starts," Jupiter said getting up from the table.

"Can I come?" Miguel asked.

"This is not for you, man."

Miguel was appalled. "Why not? You think I'm too soft or something?"

Jupiter smiled. "You talk too much."

"What do you mean? I haven't said anything to anybody."

Jupiter just stared at him.

Miguel was miffed, trying to figure out what he was referring to. "I know you're not trippin about when I told them girls at the arcade that you sold drugs."

"That's exactly what I'm talking about. You don't tell people that shit...ever. You think this is all a joke. It's not. I don't want to do this at all, let alone for a lifetime. You're my boy so I tell you, but I don't want people to judge me off of that."

"Then quit," Miguel said like it was an easy solution.

"That'll never happen. My mother owes my aunt, and I'm the collateral."

"Have you heard from your mom?"

"I gotta go. See you in next period." Jupiter walked off.

Jupiter went down the hallway, through the gym, and out the back door. When he got to the back of the school, his math teacher was there waiting.

"What took you so long?" the teacher asked.

Jupiter slit his eyes at him. "Here," he said handing off the package. "Quit giving Byron problems. Next time you don't mention my name at all. Byron is your contact. I don't want you to get hurt."

The teacher handed over the money. "Can't I get a teacher discount?"

"Yeah, when you stop doing drugs," Jupiter said rolling his eyes.

"Don't be a smart ass."

"See you next period." Jupiter turned and walked away.

⌘

In Justine's backyard, they were celebrating Penny's birthday. It was a beautiful day. It was a princess party with all the trimmings. Pink, purple, and white balloons were everywhere. They even had hired actresses dressed as princesses walking around greeting people coming to the party and taking pictures with the kids. The guests were kids from Penny's school and close associates of Justine's who had kids Penny's age. All the foster kids were told to leave and not come back until late Saturday night. Justine went all out for Penny. Penny was the daughter that she never had, and she was spoiling her with everything down to the purple princess castle cake that was as elaborate as a wedding cake. On the top of the cake was a little girl candle that looked like Penny. Penny was in ecstasy.

Jupiter, on the other hand, was there to share her joy but suspicious of Justine's motives. He felt like she was trying to take Penny away from him. After everyone sang "Happy Birthday" to Penny, she started opening her gifts. She came down to the last two gifts, which were Jupiter's and her Auntie's. She chose Jupiter's first. It was kind of obvious what he had given her by the size and packaging. You could see the handle bars piercing through the wrapping, but Penny was excited anyway. She had told Jupiter that she wanted a bike more than anything.

When she finished ripping off the wrapping paper, Penny went and hugged her big brother. "Thank you Jupiter. I love you so much."

Jupiter caught Justine looking at him with a funny smirk. She winked at him.

"Penny, open up the last gift," Justine said urging her to open her gift now.

Penny went back and started opening up the small package gift that Justine had given her. Jupiter looked on intently, wondering what it might be. The last thing he wanted was for her to outdo him in Penny's eyes.

She looked inside the box and pulled out some keys. "What's this for?" she asked at a lost.

Justine smiled. "Every princess needs a car."

Uncle Tony came out of the house carrying a pink Cadillac electric SUV. Penny screamed at the sight of it. She ran and jumped in. Her friends ran too. Jupiter smiled. Though it was a nice toy car, he didn't feel that outdone.

Justine came over to the car and gave Penny an envelope. "Penny, I want you to know that you are the daughter that I always wanted. I love you and want nothing but the best for you, and this is just a small appreciation for the joy and happiness you have brought into my life." She stretched out her arms to her. Penny got out of the car and gave her a hug.

"I love you too, Auntie."

"Open it," Justine said, wiping the tears away from her face.

Penny opened the envelope and was speechless. She held up what was in the envelope. Jupiter saw it and got mad immediately.

"That's right, we're going to Disneyland. Just you and me in California for a week."

Penny smiled. "I'm going back to California."

"Girl, you never been to California," Justine said.

Jupiter gave Penny a stern glare. Penny saw him.

"In my dreams," she replied, giving her aunt another hug. "This is the best birthday ever. Can Jupiter go with us?"

Justine and Jupiter stared at each other. "No, Jupiter can't afford to miss school. Maybe another time. I'm sure he won't mind us going by ourselves."

"Penny, you go and enjoy yourself," he said gritting his teeth.

"Are we catching the bus?" Penny asked.

Justine smirked. "Why would anybody ever catch the bus to California?" She laughed. "We're flying on a private jet," Justine said loud enough for everyone in the backyard to hear. She kissed Penny on the forehead and walked off. She met Jupiter at the door.

"That was a great gift Auntie," he said with a forced grin on his face. "Penny will enjoy Disneyland."

"Your gift was great too. Your sister is so attached to you," Justine said as if that was a problem. "She needs to trust me more."

"I'm all she knows and trusts," he said with a hint of sarcasm.

Justine smiled at him. "You two can trust me. You're the only family that I have outside of Uncle Tony and his raggedy baby mommas kids. Dumb as a doorbell. They're nothing like you and Penny. I want the best for the both of you."

"Have you heard from my mother?" he asked.

"You keep asking that same question. She's ain't coming back, and she doesn't care about either of you. Haven't you learned anything in this life," Justine said. She wanted them to forget about their mother. "Maggie never cared."

"I'm sorry, but she is our mother. Penny misses her."

"Doesn't seem like that to me," Justine said, glancing over at Penny playing with her friends and the many toys that she got for her birthday.

"She does," Jupiter said, still unsure himself.

"Maybe you're losing touch with her. Penny is thriving here. Uncle Tony has told me that you have been doing a great job for us. Having you inside the school makes moving things a lot better. Plus, you have gotten the respect from the other kids as well. You're a leader."

"I'm about to go meet Gideon at the park," Jupiter said changing the subject.

Justine grabbed him by the arm. "You watch that Gideon. Uncle Tony thinks he may be taking money off the top. Since he moved out, the money has been coming up short."

"Not Gideon. You can trust him," Jupiter said. He knew if she had confirmation, that would be the end to Gideon.

"Would you put your life on it?"

He cut his aunt a cold stare. "I'll watch him."

She grinned at him. "That's what I like to hear. Just remember the other kids here can't be a hundred percent trusted."

"Got it. Can I go now?" he asked.

"Yeah, but wait, your birthday is coming up in two months. What do you want? I know you're always talking about going to that coliseum to watch basketball, but what else?"

"Nothing, I'm good."

"Jupiter, everybody wants something for their birthday. I want you to be happy too."

"I am happy," he said, wanting her to drop the birthday discussion.

His aunt saw that he wasn't going to give her any clue to what his birthday wish was. "I'll just have to surprise you."

"You really don't," he said hoping that she wouldn't do anything. Jupiter didn't want to feel like he owed her or anybody anything when he left again.

"Go and enjoy the park. See you later." Justine turned around and headed back toward Penny.

⌘

When Jupiter got to the park, he didn't see Gideon anywhere. He started shooting baskets on the court with some other kids. About an hour had gone by when he saw a silver GLS 450 Mercedes SUV blow its horn and someone yelled his name. From the distance, Jupiter couldn't tell who was in the car. As he walked closer, the person jumped out. Too his surprise, it was Gideon smiling from ear to ear.

"Hey, youngen'," Gideon said.

Jupiter glanced in the car and saw two girls inside. "Whose car is this?" he asked admiring the vehicle.

Gideon laughed. "I just picked this up today, kid. You like?"

"From who?"

"The Mercedes dealership, fool. Where else? You like it, don't you?" Gideon grinned.

The first thing that came to mind for Jupiter was the comment his aunt made about Gideon skimming off the top. It hurt him to know that she had told him the truth. He looked at

Gideon with pity for having been so stupid to steal from his aunt.

"Please say you stole it," Jupiter said staring at him.

Gideon got offended. "Why I need to steal this? I'm young, black, and paid."

"Where did you get the money from?"

Gideon grabbed him by the arm and pulled him away from the car. "Man, forget about all that money stuff. Her friend in the back is all in. All you have to do is get in the back seat, and that's you. The head is crazy."

Jupiter looked at him like he was crazy. He couldn't believe how Gideon was avoiding the eight hundred pound gorilla standing between them.

"I can't man."

"Don't be a pussy man," Gideon said. "I got condoms."

"You know my aunt thinks you're stealing from her."

Gideon smirked. "Ain't nobody stealing from her."

"That car cost eighty thousand dollars. Last I checked, you shouldn't have that kind of money." Jupiter remember seeing that SUV being advertised in a magazine with the price next to it. He knew Gideon didn't have a credit score to buy or lease it. He could have only gotten that vehicle by paying cash up front. And that money could have only been stolen from Justine.

"So, now you checkin' my pockets?" Gideon got a little upset.

Jupiter tried to reason with him. "I'm trying to save you. Uncle Tony will kill you."

"I got a gun too." Gideon pulled out his nine millimeter gun. "Uncle Tony can't touch me. He's old."

"Man, take the car back. If you keep it, she'll find out sooner than later."

He grabbed Jupiter by the shirt. "You gonna snitch on me? I thought we were better than that."

"You work for me, Gideon. What you do affects me and everybody else." Jupiter snatched his hands off of his shirt. "I'm trying to help you."

"Look at you, little man, now you running things. I taught you all you know. I'm your boss, and you just don't know it."

Jupiter looked in his eyes and could tell by the redness that Gideon was high on something. He wanted to talk sense into him, but in his present condition, he knew that wasn't going to get far.

"Yeah, I work for you." Jupiter shook his head and walked off.

Gideon felt bad. "Jup, come back man. She wants you." He looked inside the car. "What's your name again?" he asked the girl in the backseat.

"Gina," the girl replied.

Gideon went right back to trying to get Jupiter to come back. "Gina said she wants you. You're going to leave me hanging?" He waited for a second to see if Jupiter would turn around. He didn't. "Forget you then. More bitches for me. And hell nawl, I ain't taking this bad ass car back." Gideon got in the SUV and took some ecstasy. "We about to have a ball tonight."

"What's up with your boy?" the girl in the passenger seat asked. "He too good for us, or is he gay?"

"Shut your mouth. That's my boy." Gideon started thinking about what Jupiter had said. He stared at himself in the rearview mirror. A weird feeling of regret came over him as he drove off down the street.

Jupiter had heard him and wanted to turn around, but the problem Gideon had created was bigger than the two of them. Though Gideon didn't completely know Jupiter's situation with his aunt, the confirmation of him stealing money from her would have a ripple effect on Jupiter and his relationship with Penny. And that was one relationship that nobody was worth him risking.

CHAPTER TWELVE

S chool had just ended, and Jupiter sat on the outside steps of the school talking to Miguel when Angela came over to them. Jupiter smiled at her. It was as obvious as the radiant sun that was beaming on their heads that they had a crush on each other. Angela was a dark skinned girl from his side of town, very beautiful and athletic. Most of the boys in the school had their eyes on her, but hers were strictly on Jupiter. He wanted to tell her what was in his heart. The thing that kept him from pursuing her was the life he was living. She actually lived about four blocks away from his aunt's house. But she came from a middle class household with two working parents. And to ensure that Angela didn't get caught up in the street life in their neighborhood, she wasn't allowed to be out at any time unless one of her parents was with her. It was the part of her life that she hated with a passion.

"Hey Angela," Miguel said winking at her.

She frowned at him. "You know I'm here to see your boy." She smiled at Jupiter. She reached out and handed him a card.

He looked at Miguel smugly and took the card. "What's this?" he asked while opening it.

"I'm having a birthday party, and I want you to come. My parents said I could invite you."

"Why me?" Jupiter asked.

"My parents are impressed with how smart you are."

"Thanks, but what about my boy here." He glanced at Miguel. "We're a package deal."

She sighed. Angela really wanted him to come to her party so her parents could finally meet him. She didn't tell anybody, but she had been bragging about how smart he was to her parents since they were in elementary school. Though Miguel somewhat creeped her out, she was willing to sacrifice that feeling in order to get Jupiter to her place.

"Okay, but don't be acting crazy like you do in French class. My dad doesn't play; he will kick you out without a second thought."

"Where's my invitation?" Miguel asked glancing over at Jupiter.

"I'm telling you about it. Just get the information from Jupiter."

Jupiter grinned at her. "It's not a real invite without the card. Don't do him like that."

She huffed. "Are you coming? If you are, I'll get him a card tomorrow."

Jupiter's alarm on his watch went off. "Shoot, I have to pick up my sister. Bye."

"Are you coming?" she asked again as he was walking away.

He nodded. "Wouldn't miss it for the world." He turned and ran off.

"I'll be there too," Miguel said blowing her a kiss. "I hope you got some cute friends."

She rolled her eyes at him.

"You know Jupiter's birthday is in two weeks," he said which brought a smile to her face.

"Is he having a party?" she asked.

"You won't be invited. I'll make sure of it." Miguel walked off leaving her there.

❧

Jupiter got to Penny's school rather quickly, but when he got to the playground area, he saw Penny getting in the car with Uncle Tony. From about a half block away, he tried to wave them down. As she sat in the front seat, he could see Uncle Tony putting his arm around her shoulder while they drove off. Jupiter was in fumes. With all his might, he chased the car down the street. Tired, out of breath, with no chance of catching the car, he stopped.

❧

Jupiter arrived home on a rampage to find Penny and Uncle Tony. He went through every room in the house and found nothing. They hadn't made it home yet. By his calculation, they should have been home an hour ago. Jupiter wanted to make sure that they weren't in Uncle Tony's bedroom so he went in it. As he dug around, he found so many sickening photos of naked little girls in Uncle Tony's possession. He also saw a stack of DVDs labeled for "For My Eyes Only". He couldn't take it anymore, so he walked out. Jupiter went to the front of the house and waited. They came home about thirty minutes later with ice cream cones. Jupiter didn't care if everything seemed alright, he still charged at them.

"Penny, go in the house and to your room," he said staring Uncle Tony into the ground. He was ready to battle Uncle Tony no matter what the odds were against him.

Uncle Tony threw his ice cream cone to the ground. "You want me to hurt you, don't you?" He smiled.

Jupiter didn't back down. "I told you to stay away from her."

"You don't tell me anything. This is my house." Uncle Tony came around the car and moved closer to him. He had expected Jupiter to move, but he didn't. Uncle Tony slowed his forward progression. "It's just some ice cream," Uncle Tony said.

Jupiter balled up his fist. "Just stay away from her. I'm not warning you anymore."

"Are you threatening me?" Uncle Tony laughed.

"No, I'm just telling you the facts."

From the top of the stairs, Justine came out with Penny.

"Is there a problem boys?" she glanced at them both as the tension between then got thicker.

Jupiter said nothing. He just stood there, waiting to strike.

"No problem here. Jupiter and I are just talking," Uncle Tony said to his big sister. He didn't want her to know why they were about to fight. Uncle Tony knew if Justine had any clue that he was preying on Penny that she might use deadly forces on him.

"Better be about Gideon," she said focusing solely on Jupiter.

Uncle Tony smiled. "Oh yeah, your boy done messed up now."

Justine waved them inside. "We need to discuss that situation now. Meet me in my office."

Jupiter looked in Penny's eyes. He hoped that this wouldn't be the last time that he saw her. He thought the Gideon situation had resolved itself since he hadn't heard anything else about him stealing off the top or the Mercedes Benz he had bought. Trying to figure out what they wanted to discuss and how to handle it puzzled him greatly. He knew by the tone of his aunt's voice and the devious smile on his uncle's face that whatever they were about to discuss was not something good for Gideon.

The walk down into the basement was only one flight of stairs, but it seemed to last longer than normal. Seeing Justine wink at Uncle Tony made things clear that anything about giving Gideon a break would be discussed. This was a conversation about how and when Gideon would die. This was a moment that Jupiter had feared would happen and seeing it clearly, his body ached. They all sat down in the basement around Justine's desk.

"When were you going to tell me that Gideon had flown the coop?" Justine wasted no time in getting to the point.

"What do you mean?" Jupiter played dumb. Before he showed his hand, he wanted to know what they had on Gideon, first.

"Boy, don't have this end badly for you too. If you stand with him, you stand alone. Gideon is about self," Uncle Tony said staring at Jupiter.

"Last month his numbers were the same as normal," Jupiter said defending himself and the numbers.

"His numbers should have been doubled," Justine said. "Are you keeping account?"

"I only collect, and those numbers have been the same. Check your books. I'm not lying. I promise you."

"The past couple of months, Gideon had been getting more and more product from Uncle Tony, but his numbers don't represent that."

"He has?" Jupiter asked, shocked.

Justine and Uncle Tony both nodded their heads.

"How would I know that? Uncle Tony didn't tell me that. And if Gideon is stealing, why would he tell me that?" He smirked at his aunt and uncle at how ridiculous their assumption seemed that he should have known what Gideon was doing.

Uncle Tony looked at Justine, but he held his ground. "That doesn't matter."

Justine slit her eyes at him. She couldn't believe he thought that didn't matter. "Fool, that makes all the difference in the world. You got me thinking my nephew was in cahoots with this dead man. I hoped it wasn't true."

"Auntie, I would never steal from you like that. I promise you, I didn't know Gideon was doing any of this. If I had known earlier that he was moving extra weight, I would have informed you that I was coming up short," Jupiter said.

Justine sighed. "That finishes that part of the business."

Jupiter started to stand up.

"Sit down. I'm not done." Jupiter sat back down. "Now, I hear that Gideon has bought a nice GLS 450. Been riding it all around town. Even telling people that he doesn't have to respond to me or anyone else in this family." Justine shook her head in disbelief. "He even told people he was now a boss." She chuckled.

Fear came over Jupiter's face. "I can talk to him and get him back onboard."

Uncle Tony and Justine laughed at his solution. He threw it out there but already recognized that wasn't a viable option anymore. Uncle Tony and Justine wanted Gideon obliterated for his acts of stealing and disrespect.

"This isn't a basketball team where somebody quit the team, and we are just going to let them back on. This shit doesn't work that way," Justine said with force. "He crossed a line that no longer exists."

"It's night-night," Uncle Tony chimed in with a grin. "Do you have a problem with that?"

Jupiter looked at his aunt and uncle. He knew 'night-night' meant Gideon was about to die. He also knew that if he chose the side of Gideon, he would be going 'night-night' too.

"I'm a soldier. I stand with you two," Jupiter said sternly.

Justine thought his remarks were cute. She smirked. "No baby, you're a General. Gideon is a soldier. I'm your President." With a quick glance, Justine handed the conversation over to Uncle Tony.

"Dude, Gideon was your responsibility."

"I didn't know about the extra product."

"No one's blaming you for that. The point here is that he is one of your soldiers, your problem. You need to handle that, now."

"What do you mean?" Jupiter asked like he had no idea what was going on. This was the one thing that he hoped wouldn't come of this meeting. He figured that Gideon would have to die, but he assumed that it would be by Uncle Tony or someone on that level. Knowing now that it was up to him, he grabbed the waste basket in the office and vomited into it.

Uncle Tony and Justine thought it was funny. Out of respect, they let him finish and wipe off his mouth before saying another word.

"Do I have to?" Jupiter asked, hoping to get out of it.

"If you want respect from your crew, you have to instill some fear in them. If you don't, you will have a thousand Gideon's rising up all the time. You have to look out for us and Penny," Uncle Tony said licking his lips.

His facial expression angered Jupiter. "Leave Penny out of this."

Justine got up and walked over to him. She looked down at him. "If you don't want to do this, I understand. You won't have to."

"Thanks Auntie."

"Not too fast, cowboy. If you don't, I will have you arrested for drug dealing and thrown in a juvenile detention center. You can kiss college good bye. Yeah, I know you're thinking she wouldn't hurt Penny and you're right. I love her, but I know you would hate to not know what was going on in her life. Believe me, we will forget you existed."

Jupiter sulked for a minute. He had no choice and felt hopeless. "Okay," he said with a whimper. "When?"

"Now," Uncle Tony said.

Jupiter could see the outside the basement window. "How am I going to find him? It's getting dark outside."

"Gideon won't expect you to do anything. He has this naive mindset that you two are equals." Uncle Tony pulled out a gun from his jacket holster. He handed it over to Jupiter. "Get him alone and pop him with this and run out of there. Make sure when you run out, you have on a dark hoodie. Don't want people to see you clearly."

Jupiter's hands started shaking. Having the gun in his hand made him scared and nervous. The mission that they had set for became very real. "I don't know how to use this."

Uncle Tony snatched the gun from him. He pointed it at Jupiter. That only made it worse for Jupiter. In his mind, he swore that he was about to die.

"Get up on him and shoot at least three times. You want to make sure he's dead. Alive enemies are not good for business." Uncle Tony handed the gun back to him. "Don't play around with it. It's not on safety. And don't put it on safety."

"Why?" he asked nervously.

"You think if you pull out that gun and fire it and nothing happens that Gideon is going to let you live? It doesn't work that way in these streets. It's either you or him."

Jupiter took a deep breath. "Okay, I can do it. I will go out there tonight, find him, and get this over with," Jupiter said mainly for to convince himself that he could do it.

Justine looked at her watch. "Time is ticking. Take Rico's motor bike. That will make you travel a lot faster and be able to avoid traffic when getting out of there."

Jupiter stood up and started to leave.

"See you tonight," Uncle Tony said with a big smile stuck on his face.

Jupiter walked up the stairs and went to say bye to Penny. He knew this might be the last time, so he gave her an extra special hug and kiss on the cheek. When he got on Rico's motor bike, he glanced in his inside jacket at the gun. It freaked him out, but he rode off into the evening air.

❧

It didn't take Jupiter long at all to find Gideon. He already knew Gideon was living across town in a two bedroom apartment with his new girlfriend. As he parked the motor bike down the street in some bushes, he started to sweat. This was a nightmare for him. Killing Gideon was like killing his brother, if he had one. Gideon had been a solid friend and confidant since he got to the foster home. In his mind, he just wished that Gideon had listened to him when he said to stop stealing and to return the Mercedes.

Walking down the sidewalk, Jupiter saw the Mercedes parked out front. In his mind, he played out how killing Gideon would occur as he contemplated ringing the doorbell. After a minute, he pushed the button. Immediately, one of the other foster kids answered the door. His name was Eric. Jupiter's eyes bulged out. He hadn't expected to see him there. Eric being at Gideon's created another dilemma.

"Oh shit! Who let you out of the house?" Eric asked, greeting him with a handshake and shoulder bump. Jupiter walked inside. He saw Gideon's girlfriend and another girl sitting on the couch. They were the two girls with Gideon from the park.

"Where's Gideon?" he asked.

"Gideon, your boy who you said isn't gay, is here," she said giggling with her girlfriend.

"Who you think you're talking to?" Jupiter asked, getting upset at how she referenced him. "Shut up! Don't you ever say that to me."

"What you gonna do?" she said egging him on. "Gideon, you need to check your boy."

Jupiter started to walk toward her, but Gideon came out and got between them.

"My man, what's up?" Gideon asked as he pulled him away. "Trina, you sit your ass down."

"Your girl is out of line with that gay shit. I don't play that." Jupiter was highly offended. Not one to hit girls, he still wanted to rip her neck off.

"Noted, but what got you over here on a Saturday night. Justine let you out?" Gideon asked with a smirk. "You know she be having you and Penny on lock down."

Jupiter gave him a very serious glare. "We need to talk."

"Talk," Gideon said. "About what?"

Jupiter grabbed Gideon and took him into the kitchen area to give them a little bit of privacy. "Justine and Uncle Tony both know you have been stealing from them."

"I haven't done anything," Gideon said denying the accusation. "Did you snitch?"

Jupiter wanted to beat him up for continuing to lie to him like he was stupid. "They put it together. You have been making a lot of money and not giving Justine her cut."

"Want a drink?" Gideon asked changing the subject.

"This is serious man. She's going to kill you."

He laughed. "Let her try. I got my own little soldiers now. I'm like her now, I'm a President. What Denzel say in American Gangster? I used to work for a man who had the biggest company in New York City, but he didn't own it, the white man did, so they own him, nobody owns me though. That's how I feel now. Nobody owns me. Justine can go fuck herself."

"You can't win that fight. Just leave. I will send you money. You've been one of my best friends. I don't want to lose you," Jupiter pleaded.

"I'm not scared. You think I'm going to let Uncle Tony or any of them other busters get close to me? I know how she operates. I'm smarter than her."

At that point, Jupiter cried inside. He looked at his friend and felt pity for him. "Man, she's going to win."

"What?" He laughed. "She should've sent you to kill me; that would have been the best plan."

"Just run."

"Run where?" Gideon asked turning up his lips.

"Mexico, Canada, or maybe Brazil." Jupiter kept trying to get him to just leave. The last thing he wanted was to shoot his best friend. The more they talked, he saw no other ending to their friendship besides death.

"I'm not some high school genius who can go to any college in the world. These streets are me, and I am these streets. You're the rose that grew in from the concrete. I'm just the concrete."

"You don't have to be." Jupiter slit his eyes at him. "You're limiting who you can be. Just run."

"Never. It's not going to happen in this lifetime. Justine better call the National Guard to come get me. I'm ready for war. I'm gonna put a bullet in that retarded cousin you got and see if they like that."

"This is her town. We play by her rules," Jupiter said trying to get through to his friend.

"Not for long. I've hooked up with some dudes from Little Rock, and they are giving me what I need at a great price. I don't need Justine. In a minute Justine gonna need me. They gave me a storage locker full of guns and a hundred thousand dollars worth of drugs on credit. I'm about to be the man. With the price I'm getting for my shit, I'll be taking over her network of finger fuckers soon."

"You sure you can trust these dudes?" Jupiter asked, curious about the connection that Gideon had made.

"I'm just moving weight at a better cost to the street hustler. That's all they care about," Gideon said with a smile. "I know you want out. I got a spot at the top for you. We can run this town."

Jupiter smiled at him. The offer was tempting, but he had too much to lose if he didn't complete what Justine and Uncle Tony wanted. "Yeah, I think I will take that drink."

Gideon laughed. "Can I see your ID, young man?" He joked. He saw a sorrowful look on Jupiter's face. "No matter what, we will always be friends."

"I know," Jupiter replied back as Gideon turned to look in the refrigerator. Sweat poured down Jupiter's face.

When Gideon turned back around, Jupiter had the nine millimeter gun that Uncle Tony had given him pointed directly at his head.

"Well played," Gideon said as tears rolled down his face. "Make it quick."

"I love you Gideon," he said as he closed his eyes and fired a bullet into his head. Gideon fell to the ground.

Jupiter cried, but that was short lived. The others ran into the kitchen. At first, Jupiter didn't know what to do, but when one of the girls mentioned calling the police, and he saw Eric reach for the knife by the microwave, he did what he thought best. He shot Gideon's girlfriend, her friend, and Eric with precision. He searched Gideon's bedroom and found a large duffle bag filled with cash. He took the money, Gideon's phone, and his keys. With his hoodie over his head, he ran out the door and down the street. Jupiter got on the motor bike and rode it around the city for a few hours, crying at what he had just done. When he got near the river, he tossed the gun over the bridge into the river. He stayed there by the water in misery, thinking about the things he had done since coming to live with his aunt and uncle. He prayed for better days to come, but Jupiter was smart enough to know that those days were lost. Jupiter knew that in order for him live somewhat of a normal life, he would have to beat his aunt and uncle at their own game.

He looked in the duffle bag that he got from Gideon's place. From his point of view, he estimated that there was at least two hundred thousand dollars. Jupiter quickly rode over to his hiding spot in the sewer and put the money with the rest he had stashed away.

≼

Early the next morning, Jupiter arrived back at the house. He walked in and saw a somber look on all of the foster kids' faces as they huddled around the t.v. in the living room.

"What's going on?" he asked.

"Somebody killed Gideon and Eric last night," one foster boy said in tears. "They didn't harm anybody. I want to kill the person who did it."

Jupiter looked around the room and he saw Penny was crying as well. She had formed a bond with Gideon just like he had. He went over to his sister and gave her a hug.

"Penny, it will be alright."

She looked at him. "Why would someone do this? That person should die for this."

Jupiter released his embrace. "I'm going to take a nap."

"Uncle Tony is looking for you," she said.

"For what?" he asked a bit paranoid.

"I don't know."

"Where is he at?" Jupiter asked, wondering what he wanted now.

"I saw him go to the basement with Auntie."

"Thanks," he said, heading toward the basement.

As he went downstairs, he saw Justine's office door was open. Jupiter walked to the doorway and stood. Justine saw him standing.

"Come on in," she said smiling. "My boy."

Jupiter walked in and stood in the corner. He saw Uncle Tony sitting in the chair across from her.

"You wanted to see me?" he asked, keeping his eyes on their hands.

"You earned some serious stripes last night. I lost big money betting against you. I won't do that again," Uncle Tony said cynically.

"Pay no attention to him. I'm glad you're alive and the job is done. But why the others?" Justine asked.

"I didn't want to leave witnesses."

"Good thinking," she said, glancing over at Uncle Tony. "Eric was in on it, too."

"I never trusted that kid," Uncle Tony said smirking. "Should have left him at the group home. He wasn't worth a dime."

"Worth more than a dime now. Glad I put a quarter of a million on both of them." Justine laughed.

Jupiter couldn't believe what he was hearing. Knowing that she had life insurance on them only convinced him that he needed to do something soon in order to avoid getting deeper into the criminal life.

"Where's my gun?" Uncle Tony asked.

"In the river."

"Good thinking. We don't need that weapon coming back to haunt any of us." Justine grinned at him with her approval.

Uncle Tony frowned at Jupiter. He despised the golden boy treatment he felt Jupiter was getting.

"I have some homework I need to finish by tomorrow morning. Can I be excused?"

Justine smiled at him. "I like that work ethic. Hold on for a second, Jupiter, don't make any plans for your birthday. I have a surprise for you."

"You don't have to," Jupiter said, wishing that she hadn't planned anything for him. "I got so much school work to do."

"Too late," she said smiling at him.

CHAPTER THIRTEEN

J upiter's sixteenth birthday had finally arrived. He had tried to keep it as low profile as possible. That all changed during the last period of the day. As he was walking to his chemistry class, he noticed that the hallway going to the class was empty. When he got to the door, his teacher met him. He thought that was real weird.

"Jupiter, class today is in the gym. Follow me."

"What?" he asked. "Why?"

"Our class is being fumigated. Just follow me," she said leading the way.

Jupiter followed, still wondering if his teacher was trying to pull a fast one over on him. They got to the gym, and she opened the door for him. When Jupiter walked inside, he saw all of his classmates standing around a half globe cake of the world. He laughed until he saw his aunt standing there as well. She stepped forward.

Justine went and gave him a big hug. He had no clue to what she was up to but suspected he wouldn't like it. "My dear nephew, I love you so much. You gave me life where death once existed. This is just a small appreciation for you being you. Come on out boys," she yelled.

He didn't know who she was referring to when she said 'come on out boys'. Jupiter turned around to see who she was talking about. When he saw the entire Memphis Grizzlies basketball team come out, he almost fainted. His aunt had to hold him up while they sang happy birthday to him. In the crowd, Jupiter noticed that his friend Miguel didn't join in on the birthday singing. After the basketball players finished, their coach grabbed the microphone.

"Jupiter, we hear you are our number one fan. We need people like you at the games to cheer us on to victory. So, we are giving you low level seats for two for the rest of the season, but for tonight... I see you're getting excited," the coach said. "For tonight, you and twenty of your family and friends are celebrating your birthday in the owner's private box. I don't even think I've been there."

Jupiter turned to his aunt. "Really! Really!" She nodded her head at him. "Auntie, thank you so much. This means everything to me."

"You deserve this baby, you truly do."

He gave his aunt a big hug and, with her coaxing, he went and thanked the coach and the players for coming out and for the gift. Though he still didn't trust his aunt, this gift was a bridge that could potentially close the gap. He wondered why she was being so nice to him. He knew it wasn't for what he did in getting Gideon out of the way. But no matter what her motives were, he was not going to let that get in his way of enjoying this day or his best gift ever. As they started to cut the cake, he saw Miguel leave as Angela came to his side. Justine was impressed by how well-mannered and good looking she was.

"Aren't you going to introduce me to your aunt?" Angela asked gently brushing up against him.

Jupiter hadn't planned on it and really didn't want to. He liked having his school and home life separate.

"Auntie, this is Angela. Angela this is my aunt, Miss Jones."

"Nice meeting you Miss Jones. Jupiter is such a nice guy."

Justine smiled. "Aren't you something special? Jupiter better snatch you up."

"Angela's not my girlfriend," he said to his aunt.

Angela looked at Justine and smiled. "He could be." They shared a giggle.

"I like her. A girl who knows what she wants. 'A closed mouth never gets fed' is my philosophy."

"Can we change the subject? Here, take some cake." He handed his aunt a slice of cake.

"She's a cutie," Justine whispered in his ear.

He sheepishly smiled. "I'm a student first."

Justine was going to say more but cut herself short when she saw one of the players waving her to come over.

"Baby, I'll be right back. Treat my new friend Angela right."

The normalcy of the relationship went back to mistrust. Jupiter thought back to all the times that they threatened him with doing something to Penny. He figured if he let Angela into his life that his aunt would use that against him. The only difference would be that they would probably follow through with killing her if he didn't deliver whatever they wanted.

"Maybe we can go to the movies sometime?" Angela asked.

"Maybe," he said back to her. "You want to come to the game tonight?"

"Sure. Thanks." She kissed him on the cheek. "Happy birthday, Jupiter."

The sign of affection got the best of him. He started stuttering. "I um, I thank, thank you." He glanced into her eyes and drifted off to another world. He saw a life where he was free from all the drugs and the killings. A world where he was able to achieve his dreams.

"Are you okay, Jupiter?" she asked with a twinkle in her eye. Her desire was to kiss him on his thick lips, but that was too much of a gamble. She wasn't willing to face rejection if that was the case, though Jupiter seemed willing.

"I'm cool. Where did Miguel go?" he asked.

"That's your boy. I think he was a little jealous. He goes to those games all the time with his dad but hasn't had this type of treatment."

"Yeah, this was a little over the top. My aunt is weird like that."

"I think this was great. She loves you. It takes a lot to plan this out. And if you didn't care for that person, you wouldn't. Let people be jealous. Who cares? I like it."

Jupiter smiled. She made him feel good about himself. "I guess I'll catch up with him later." Justine came back over to them. "Are you about ready to go? We have to pick up Penny and then take you to another surprise before the game."

Angela grinned at him. She was so excited for him. She rubbed him on his back gently.

Justine saw her excitement. "Do you want to join us?"

"No," Jupiter said quickly.

Angela gave him a weird glare.

"I mean no, Angela has piano lessons after school. She said she would come to the game tonight. I got a ticket for your dad too."

"Thanks," Angela said giving him a hug. "My dad loves the Grizzlies."

"Hey, Auntie, I'll meet you at the car. I have to go invite my best friend and a couple of others."

"Don't forget that Penny and I would like to come," Justine said like he had a choice.

"Definitely! See you tonight, Angela. Bye," he said, dashing off.

Jupiter caught up with Miguel at his locker. Miguel turned around.

"What's wrong man?" Jupiter asked.

"Nothing."

Jupiter could tell something was bothering his friend. "Are you sure everything is okay? You left out of the gym before the cake."

Miguel glanced at his watch. "I gotta go."

"Really?"

"Really!" Miguel said, closing up his backpack. "My dad is outside."

"I want you to come to the game with me tonight. The owner's box."

"I don't know man," Miguel said.

Jupiter got upset. He got close up into Miguel's face. "You gonna bitch up on me now. I've been trying to go to a game for a while now, and you kept playing around like your dad couldn't get an extra ticket. Now that I got some juice you want to act like this. Are you my friend or my foe? Just say the word, and we can act accordingly."

Miguel saw the demons in Jupiter's eyes. He knew Jupiter was not a guy to have as an enemy. Though he was still very jealous, he sucked it up.

"Friend. That will never change."

"So are you coming tonight?" Jupiter asked again.

"Of course, count me in."

"Better get outside before your father leaves you," Jupiter said with a smile.

Miguel slowly walked off.

❧

Driving down the street in the limousine, Justine told her driver to pull over at the bank. Jupiter looked up and saw that it was the same one that his mother and Clyde had robbed before she disappeared on them. He was at a loss trying to figure out why they were stopping.

The limo stopped in front.

"Let's get out," she said to Penny and Jupiter.

They all walked in the bank. Justine led them over to her private banker. They went in his office and sat down.

"Happy birthday," the banker said to Jupiter. "Sixteen is a great age."

"Thanks," he said trying to understand why they were there.

Justine smiled. "You're wondering what's going on, huh?"

He shook his head yes.

The banker slid a check book, savings account book, and a debit card with his name on it to him. "Look at it," the banker said.

Jupiter looked inside the books.

"That's right. You have two hundred and fifty thousand dollars now. All yours. I am giving you this for your college fund, not that you will need it. You will definitely be getting a full scholarship."

"I don't know about that," he said.

"Please, all you have to do is get a good score on your SAT and finish strong next year in school. You're going to be this family's first college graduate. When do you take the SAT?"

"In a month."

She grabbed his hand and held it. "I'm giving you this money so that you never have to worry about anything. I know you're smart enough to manage it."

He smiled as his eyes became intertwined with the numbers. Jupiter was at a loss on what to say. His birthday had turned out to be something way more than even his dreams.

"This is all mine?" he asked, curious if he could withdraw from it at any time.

"All yours, you can take from this account whenever you want. I have no control over this, do I?" she glanced at the banker.

The banker shook his head no.

"Is Jupiter now rich?" Penny said, getting a laugh from everybody in the room.

"Close to it," the banker said.

"Next stop, the game," Justine said, getting up from her seat.

❧

That night, all of Jupiter's close friends made it. From his family, only his aunt and Penny were there, which satisfied him greatly. Since, he didn't like his uncle or cousin, their non-appearance made it even more special. Now that they were up in owner's box, Miguel seemed to soften his jealous stance. He was just as excited as everyone else. They had all the trimmings they wanted. It was an amazing evening that Jupiter would never forget. He had a newfound respect for his aunt. It seemed as if their relationship was turning a corner for the good. It wasn't until Miguel's father saw them from his low level section seat that the night changed. He came up to the box area and demanded that he be let inside to get his son. The security told

Justine what was going on. She went outside to talk to his father.

"You get my son out of there right now. We don't socialize with criminals," his father said pointing his finger at Justine.

She walked closer to him. "You need to lower your voice now."

"You don't control me. I know who you are and what you're about. You're dirt. The scum of the earth. I can step on you." Miguel's father then did something that would change his life forever; he poked Justine in the chest with his index finger.

Justine had to bite her tongue. She had visions of scratching his eyes out. "Now you have cancelled Christmas." She walked back into the room. She went over to Miguel. "Miguel, thanks for coming, but your father is waiting for you outside."

"Can't he come inside?" Miguel asked. He didn't want to leave the party.

"I wish he could, but that's not an option," Justine said trying to keep a calm composure. "Your father wants you to leave."

Jupiter saw his aunt talking to Miguel and came over. "Is everything alright?" He could tell his aunt was upset.

"Miguel's father wants him to come out. He needs to go now." Justine gave Jupiter a sorrowful look. "He hit me," she said gritting her teeth. "Nobody ever puts their filthy paws on me."

"Miguel, thanks for coming. I'll see you at school. Bye, man." He gave his friend a pound. Miguel walked out and was immediately snatched up by his father and dragged off. His father was screaming and yelling all the way through the building and to their car.

Back inside the party, Justine stepped outside the door and made a call. "Yes, I need some trash taken out."

"When?" Uncle Tony asked on the other end.

"Not tonight. I need you to find out everything you know about a Sylvester Thomas. He was way too flippant at the mouth to be some normal everyday joker."

"What happened?"

"I'll tell you later. I just wanted to tell you so that you get a head start on digging up his dirt."

"I got you sis. Then after that, we will burn him like never before."

"I'm definitely burning his house of cards down to the ground," she said, looking down at where he had poked her in the chest. It still bugged her that he had the audacity to do it. It took every strength within her to not want to kill him tonight. Being a pragmatic person, she knew better than to let her first emotion run how she handled the situation. She had built her successful crime organization on out-thinking the best thinkers. And in no way was this incident going to change her process.

When Uncle Tony hung up the phone, Jabari came into his father's office in the basement. Uncle Tony had been drinking and for a moment just stared at his son with disappointment. Jabari took a seat across from him.

"Why Auntie spend so much money on Jupiter? He ain't nothing special. What about me, Pops? She had the whole Memphis Grizzlies at the school singing happy birthday to that fool."

"What about you?" Uncle Tony slit his eyes at his son.

"I'm just saying, before he came to the house, Auntie Justine didn't care at all about him or his little sister. We don't even know them," Jabari said indignantly. "He ain't that smart."

"Smarter than you, apparently. You need to buck the fuck up and do something deserving."

"I can sell a little something at school or on the streets?"

"Have you lost your damn mind?" Jabari shrugged his shoulders. "You don't have it in you to sell drugs. Your momma made you too soft for this shit," Uncle Tony said. "Jupiter is the next king of these streets."

"I'm better than Jupiter!"

"Prove it!"

"How? You won't let me sell anything," Jabari said, confused by what his father wanted him to do.

"Be a better student. Deserve the shit I buy you. But most of all, I want you to be my eyes and ears on Jupiter," Uncle Tony said. "I don't trust him. I still think he was involved with that Gideon kid."

"Me too," Jabari said,. "Pop, why don't you teach me the business? You and Auntie both taught him the game."

"Your aunt Maggie has a debt he's working off. If he dies, that shit don't mean nothing to me. You're my son, you're above this shit!"

"I just want to be more. He gets all these people respecting him. Give me a chance?" Jabari begged.

Uncle Tony didn't know what to say to his son. On one hand, he wanted to get him more involved, but on the other hand, he knew his son didn't have the temperament to move and adapt to the rapid change in the drug game. The last thing he wanted was to bury his only son.

"You're going to college, and this is the last time we're talking about it!"

Jabari saw the seriousness in his father's face and shut down his own pursuit of being involved in the drug game.

CHAPTER FOURTEEN

I t was a late night Friday by the docks. Rain poured down hard, making it difficult to see. Pulling up in the black Chevy Suburban SUV was Uncle Tony, Justine, and Jupiter with two bodyguards driving. Behind them were two more black Suburbans that were a part of their caravan. As the SUVs stopped, they sat waiting. In the backseat, Jupiter was studying his SAT book.

"Are you ready for your test tomorrow?" Justine asked. "I'm sure you're going to do great."

Jupiter was deep in thought on the reading comprehension section. He heard, but hated that she had brought him out here with them so he stayed quiet.

Justine could tell that he was mad. She wouldn't have brought him if it wasn't for her desire to show him all facets of the business. Her eyes glared at him.

"Boy, I know you hear her speaking to you," Uncle Tony said raising his voice.

"Let him study Tony. He's our future," she said smiling.

Jupiter hated that she kept referencing him as the future. In his mind, he just wanted to graduate high school, go to college, and leave Memphis with his sister forever. The drug dealing part of his life was something he definitely was going to put in his past.

"I'm sorry, what did you say Auntie?" he asked Justine.

"Nothing. I just want to make sure you understand our entire operation."

He looked up at her. "I'm paying close attention. I'm trying to figure out my timing so that I can finish the test in enough time. I have to be in the top percentile in order to get into Harvard or Yale or Stanford."

"Man, I remember getting a thirty-five hundred score on the SAT. Top that!" Uncle Tony said smirking.

"Tony, quit lying," Justine said rolling her eyes. "The score range is between six hundred and twenty four hundred. No way could you have scored higher than six hundred. You dropped out of high school. Why do you hate Jupiter so much? Quit hating."

"Don't nobody like that punk. He just gets on my nerves," Uncle Tony muttered .

"Sounds like hate," Justine said winking over at Jupiter, who smiled. She glanced down at her watch. "Where are they at? They're late by over fifteen minutes. That's unusual for Donte."

"They haven't called to say things have changed. Let's give them five more minutes." Uncle Tony looked out the window to see if they were coming.

"Did you get that information I requested a while ago?" she asked staring at him.

"Not yet. My people downtown can't find any record of him anywhere."

Justine paused for a moment thinking about what that meant. "Federal agent?"

"Might be."

Justine looked at Jupiter. "By the way, what does your friend Miguel's father do?"

Jupiter shrugged his shoulders. "I think he does something for the government. Why?"

"Just wondering. He didn't want to socialize with us doing your party. And then he put his hands on me."

Two black unmarked cargo vans pulled up in front of them.

"They made it," Uncle Tony said with a grin. "I told you Donte would come through."

The cargo vans flashed their lights. Justine's people in the other two Suburbans got out. Within a second, multiple shots were fired from the cargo vans killing Justine's people. Her driver was shot, but he was able to drive the car away from the docks. Justine, Uncle Tony, and Jupiter ducked down trying to not get shot. They got away and parked in a dark alley. The bodyguard in the passenger seat was dead, and the driver was shot in the shoulder. He was bleeding badly. Justine was losing it. Uncle Tony was getting paranoid as they sat. Jupiter was in shock as blood dripped from his head.

Justine noticed blood coming down Jupiter's face. She screamed and checked him out. "Oh, no, oh, no, are you okay? Did you get shot?" she asked the incoherent Jupiter.

Jupiter slowly took his hand and touched where the blood was coming from. He looked at the blood in his hand. "I'm dying?" he asked as tears raced down his face.

"No. The bullet grazed you. You're going to be okay," Justine said reassuringly. "We're going to get you taken care of now. Uncle Tony, take us to Harold's place. He'll take care of all this." She struggled, but Justine didn't break down.

For the first time since knowing her, Jupiter saw her fearful. He knew now that her reign on top had competition, and his goal was to figure out who should align with them, so that he could find a way out of this life for good.

Uncle Tony jumped out of the car. He threw the passenger out of the SUV, told the driver to switch and jumped in the driver seat. He drove off quickly.

❧

Early the next morning, Uncle Tony dropped Jupiter off at school for his SAT test. Jupiter's head was bandaged up, covering the scratch he received from being nearly shot. He got out of the car and didn't look back. He closed his eyes to refocus for the test. Scoring high on the test was the start of his plan to get out of the life he currently had. In the back of his mind was the thought of who was bad enough to make an attempt on his aunt's life. He kind of wished the person was successful, but knew that would have meant his death as well. Whoever they were, Jupiter wanted to know them.

"Bye fool. Bad luck," Uncle Tony said, driving off giving him the middle finger.

❧

Back in Justine's basement, which now seemed more like a bunker, she had security around the clock guarding the premises. Her nerves were so bad that her hands kept shaking. During her rise to the top, no one had ever come that close to killing her. It puzzled her thinking about who it might have been. All the usual suspects were either too weak, too dumb, in jail, or dead. She had grown even more frustrated that Uncle Tony was of little help. He was like a lost child, expecting her to provide all the answers.

Uncle Tony stood up. "Maybe it was Sam Daniel's and his crew?"

Justine stared down on her desk. She looked up at him. "Are you kidding me? Tell me you're joking?"

"What?" he asked clueless to what she was referring to.

"That is the third time you mentioned Sam. He is not going to come up against me. I have been supporting his family since he got locked up. Whoever that was last night, they are not from here and don't care about rules. I need to know who they are right now. And when are you going to tell me who the hell Sylvester Thomas is?" she asked raising her voice. "I need results. People are trying to kill us, and you aren't helping at all."

"He's a federal agent."

"You wait to tell me this shit now?" Justine picked up the globe paper weight and threw it at him. He barely got out of the way.

"I just found out today," Uncle Tony said, trying to plead his case. She wasn't buying it.

"We've been sitting here talking for over an hour." Justine took a deep breath. "What does he have on us?"

"Nothing."

"How do you know that?" It didn't seem right to her that he didn't know anything.

"CJ got the information from an agent he got on the inside. Sylvester has been tracking us for over ten years and has come up with nothing."

"What about his son?"

"What about him?" Uncle Tony asked nonchalantly.

"Do you think he could be working Jupiter for information?" Justine was trying hard to think of what Sylvester's move could be.

"I doubt it," Uncle Tony said. "You know I don't trust anybody, and even I definitely think you're stretching it there."

"Maybe, but we can't afford to make costly mistakes. Maybe it's time for our exit strategy." She stared across the table at her brother as she cleared the lump in her throat.

He chuckled. "You're kidding right?"

She didn't flinch.

"Justine, what else are we going to do? You're not even fifty. Travel? Done that. Been around the world five times. There's nothing in the world that we're good at besides what we do now."

"Somebody wants us dead. Or at least me. Last night was the first time I realized that I don't want to die yet." Justine got emotional. This was an unusual sight for Uncle Tony. She had always been somewhat distant and cold, never letting her family see her soft side. The time she had spent with Penny had made her soft and released the hard exterior she typically showed to people.

"I knew this was going to happen," Uncle Tony said menacingly. "You let that little girl get to you. Justine, this is not the time to quit what we've built. We need to find who's responsible for last night and get rid of them with the quickness."

Justine glanced down at her watch. "What time is Jupiter's test over?"

Uncle Tony rolled his eyes. "You and them damn kids again. I'm not dying over you getting soft. You need to buck up sis, we're going to war."

"But with who, Tony? You're fighting an invisible man."

"At least I'm fighting."

She stopped talking and closed her eyes. After taking a deep breath, her eyes opened again. "Okay, Tony, you want to go to war then let's go to war. First thing first, you need to get rid of Sylvester Thomas. We can't win anything if we're fighting multiple opponents. He has to die soon. Find him and kill him."

"What are you going to do?" Uncle Tony asked, feeling like he was the one doing the heavy lifting.

"I'm going to find and kill the people who tried to kill us last night. Do you have a problem with that?" she said forcefully to him. "Go pick up Jupiter now!"

"Why you getting mad at me?"

She smirked at him. "Because I can! You work for me."

Uncle Tony was pissed, but got up and quietly left her office.

✍

In a warehouse downtown on Beale Street, Uncle Tony and Justine walked inside. They couldn't believe their eyes seeing Clyde tied up in front of them. It was almost comical, but nobody laughed. By the way Clyde looked, it was obvious that he had been worked over a bit by the people who found him. He sat there staring at Uncle Tony and Justine with disdain.

"Clyde the Glide, with nobody by his side," Uncle Tony said shaking his head. "The prodigal son returns."

Uncle Tony's comment got a laugh out of everyone there, except for Clyde.

Justine sat in the chair in front of him. "Where is Maggie?"

Clyde didn't respond. He just rolled his eyes.

Justine looked at the people who found him. "What's the story?"

"We found him at his cousin's house on the east side visiting his momma. This fool came back for a family reunion," one of the capturers said.

Justine grinned. "What about the family?"

"What about the family?" the capturer said back to her. "The bounty was one hundred thousand for him. They were just in the way."

Clyde turned to the capturer. "Let me go, I swear you're a dead man."

"Where's my sister, Clyde?" Justine asked.

Clyde ignored her again. Uncle Tony came over and hit him in the forehead with his pistol. It knocked Clyde out of his seat.

"I ain't telling you shit!" he said from the ground.

Justine sighed. "Yeah, Maggie definitely wasn't at your momma's house. She hated her. She's too smart to come back here with you and risk getting caught. My sister isn't that dumb. Dumb enough to listen to you, but smart enough to not follow you into hell. But she is in the states."

"Clyde don't roll on nobody. I'm a Gangster Disciple. You kill me, and you got hell to pay. You don't want a war. Darius will kill you."

"Everyone is a part of my family, not yours. I run this town. GDs, Vice Lords, La Raza Nation, Crips, Bloods, and whoever else you name sits at my table. I'm standing tall while you lay in the dirt. Darius likes living. You're all alone on this trip."

"We'll see!" Clyde said, looking up at her still with an air confidence.

Justine thought about his words of wisdom. "I told you a while ago, Clyde, that nobody cares about you. You think we found you by accident? Who you think gave you up?"

"They wouldn't do that," Clyde said proudly. "Not Darius."

"They wanted their cut of the money too. I gave it to them. This is the best investment of my life. Seeing you dead makes the money worthless. Like you."

"You need me."

"You've been dead to me since the day I met you. Once you're dead, my sister will come back seeking revenge." Justine slit her eyes at him. "You're just the appetizer."

Clyde saw his death was unavoidable. "What do you want?" he asked begging. "Clyde will tell you whatever you want."

Justine looked over at Uncle Tony. "Put this nigga to sleep!" she said turning away and walking toward the exit as Uncle Tony pulled out his switch blade and slit Clyde's throat.

❧

A few days had gone by since the killing of Clyde, when the news of his death hit the news channels. Jupiter and Penny sat in front of the television, spellbound. Seeing Clyde's face pasted all over the news was surreal. They intently waited to hear if their mother was with him or even caught.

"Does that mean Mommy is dead too?" Penny asked her brother.

Jupiter didn't know how to respond to her. He had thought that Clyde and his mother would remain gone for the rest of their lives. It was an idea he had grown comfortable with.

"I don't think so," he said leery of his own statement. He didn't want to lie to his sister and later find out that their mother was also dead.

"What happened? When did Uncle Clyde rob a bank?"

He turned to his sister. "Someone killed him." In the back of his mind, he knew who did. It was just a matter of proving it.

"Why?" Penny began crying. He hugged her.

"It's going to be alright, Penny. I'm here for you," he said comforting her.

Penny surprisingly moved away from him. "I'm going to see Auntie."

"What do you mean? We're a team. You don't need her like that, Penny." Jupiter slit his eyes at her. Her favoring Justine over him was disturbing to him.

"But I love her, Jupiter. Just like I love you. She's nice to me." Penny started to walk off.

He grabbed her by the arm. "You're not going anywhere."

"You're hurting me, Jupiter. Auntie's never hurts me," Penny said looking into his eyes. "She's always nice to me."

He saw the pain and stopped clutching her arm. "I'm sorry," he said. "Penny, I need you to know I'm all you got."

"I love Auntie. She told me I don't have to listen to you anymore. You're not my mother or father."

It felt like a knife was cutting up his gut. "She told you that!"

"Yeah. You're just my brother."

"Go Penny, we'll talk later," he said wanting her to get out of his face. He didn't want her to see his anger emerge.

Penny left the room. Jupiter got up and took a walk.

He walked for almost two hours. The evening had shifted to night, and he found himself sitting on a bench at Tom Lee Park. While thinking about his mom, Gideon, Penny, and what he could do to get out of his predicament, three dark strangers walked up to him. He looked at them, waiting on their next

132

move. By their stance, they had evil intentions until one of the men recognized Jupiter.

"Jupiter, is that you?" the man said as he walked out of the darkness and into the shimmering park light.

Jupiter saw his face and smiled. He pointed at the guy, but couldn't remember his name. "You're Clyde's cousin."

"Darius."

"I'm sorry, Darius," Jupiter said.

"No problem man. I take it you heard about Clyde dying," Darius said, taking a seat next to him on the park bench. "Hey fellas, give me and the little man some privacy." His two friends lit up a joint and walked deeper into the park.

"I'm sorry about your cousin. Was my mother with him?"

"No, Clyde came home for our family reunion alone. He didn't say anything about Maggie. I told him to not come home until I straightened things out with Justine. And she goes out there and kills him. That bitch killed a lot of my people."

"She killed him?" Jupiter was surprised.

"Who else could have done that to him? Then she and Uncle Tony were out there telling some lie about some white dudes who kidnapped you probably killed him."

"Really?"

Darius stared in his face. "Did some white boys kidnap you and your sister?"

His pain was visible, and Jupiter wanted to help by telling the truth. He just wasn't sure that he could trust Darius. With Darius now being the head of the Gangster Disciples, Jupiter didn't know where his loyalties rested. "Yes."

Darius shook his head. "I still think it was her and that evil ass Uncle Tony. If I find out different, I'm killing everybody. Clyde wasn't perfect, but he's my family. My aunt and uncle were in the house when they took him." Darius got emotional. "They killed them in cold blood."

"Sorry to hear that. Clyde was a good dude, sometimes," Jupiter said trying to read Darius. "My mom really loved him."

"Little man, I also heard you were running the streets now for Justine. What about school? You used to be smart as a whip. Don't let her ruin your life."

"I'm still going to school. Justine has me paying for what my mom and Clyde did to her."

"Who said slavery was dead? She's a trip." He looked towards the direction his friends had gone. "I better get out of here. You still getting straight A's like Indian hair?"

They both laughed.

"Haven't stopped," Jupiter said grinning at him.

"You know I got your back whenever you need me. Clyde was your people too, and that makes you my people." Darius stood up and gave him a hug. "Be strong young black man," he said as he slowly walked away into the night air of the park.

Jupiter sat there pondering his fate. Part of him wished he had told Darius the truth about the kidnapping farce. Then he remembered what Gideon told him about the guys from Little Rock and how they were willing to supply him drugs at a lower cost than normal for distribution. His mind started to think that if he got the drugs at a lower cost, he could supply the gangs and the corner dealers at a lower cost and force them to stop their deal with Justine. He thought about chasing down Darius in the park, but needed his plan to be fully baked before enlisting anyone else's help.

"I got to get that number," he said heading off to his sewer hiding spot.

❧

The following week in the lunch room, Jupiter sat alone until Miguel came to sit down with him. Jupiter glanced up at him. His first thought was to tell Miguel that he didn't want to be bothered and to not sit down then he remembered how Justine had asked him about what Miguel's father did for a living. Jupiter figured that his aunt, for some reason, considered Miguel's father a threat. As he thought about it, he wanted to know himself exactly what his father did too.

"What's up Miguel?" Jupiter asked giving him a warm welcome. "Take a seat."

Miguel wondered why Jupiter was being extra nice, but still took a seat across from him. "Are you okay?"

"I'm sorry about the past couple of days. I was tripping. The SAT and almost being shot messed me up. I was thinking crazy. We good?" He stuck out his fist out for Miguel to give him a fist bump, which Miguel did.

"Yeah man, you were tripping. Did your family figure out who did it?"

He shook his head. "Nope. My aunt has the house on lockdown. She's even patting the others down when they come in the house. It's really got her spooked."

"I don't know how you can live like that," Miguel said starting to eat.

"By the way man, have you told anybody what I've told you about my family?" Jupiter stared into his face. He wanted to catch any signs of Miguel lying.

"No, of course not."

"Are you sure about that? Nobody?"

The pressure mounted on Miguel as he was faced with answering the question again. "Never."

There was a long pause as Jupiter stretched his neck. "I didn't think you did. I just need to know who I can trust and who can keep their mouth shut. I've been thinking I can't go through this next year. I want to go to college. I want to live a normal life." Jupiter sucked it up. Deep down he wanted to cry in front of his friend.

"So what are you going to do?"

"I don't know. I just want out of this life," Jupiter said. "Your father works for the government, do you think he can help?"

Miguel bit his bottom lip. He didn't want to answer that question. Seeing Jupiter be open and honest, he wanted to help his friend out the best way possible. "I don't think so. My father does like counter-terrorism or something like that. He used to be a colonel in the military."

"Counter-terrorism in Memphis?"

"I don't know. I don't ask, and he doesn't tell. My mom hates his job. It's like they are both sworn to secrecy."

Jupiter sighed. By Miguel's responses it confirmed that his father was an undercover agent. He now needed to use that to his advantage. "I think I have a way out of all this."

Miguel was surprised by the quick turnaround. "What are you going to do?"

Jupiter leaned forward across the table and whispered. "I'm going to fight fire with fire. I'm going to start my own family."

Miguel's eyes grew big. "Are you fuckin' crazy? That's not helping you get out. Just wait and graduate then you will be free. You're not a crime boss. You're just a kid in high school."

Jupiter rolled his eyes. "You think I will ever be free?"

"You're probably going to Harvard or Stanford. Those places are far from here." Miguel thought he had given Jupiter the response he needed. "It's very simple."

"You think they are going to let me take Penny with me? Hell no. My aunt and uncle know I won't leave her behind. Penny's my only real family." He covered his face with his hands out of frustration.

"How are you planning to start this crime family that's going to go up against your aunt's?" He gave Jupiter a weird stare to represent how stupid he thought the idea was.

Jupiter faced him. "I have over half a million dollars in cash..."

"What the hell?" Miguel couldn't believe he had that much money. "How did you get that much? Did you have to kill somebody?" He smirked in a joking fashion.

Flashing thoughts of killing Gideon and the others at his place entered his mind. He quickly blocked them out. "I've put money up. My aunt gave me two hundred and fifty thousand as a college fund and the rest came from me doing what I do."

"I don't know Jupiter. That's a dangerous move. I know you're doing it now, but this kind of move is not a get rich or die trying move. It's all die trying. If your aunt or uncle finds out, you're dead. And then what about Penny?"

"Penny will be okay if I get caught, but if I do nothing, my life is ruined. I'm doing it. I already got a crew. I just need to become the new distributor offering a cheaper price. I got someone to supply me out of Little Rock. I met them last night."

"You really got half a million dollars?" Miguel was still in disbelief.

"Man, that's not important," Jupiter said. "Focus."

"How you know these people?"

"Gideon told me about them before he died," Jupiter said looking away. He tried his best to hide his guilt. "I got their contact when Gideon was trying to recruit me to join him."

"Do you think you can trust them?"

"Not in this business." Jupiter smiled. "Never trust anybody."

"Why not?" Miguel asked.

"It's kind of complicated, but it's not a wise move to trust someone in a criminal organization." Jupiter's trepidation was written all over his face.

"Do you have a choice?"

"I know. With my money, I can buy from them and sell to the dealers on the street. It shouldn't take but about six months for me to build up."

"Build up what? From what you tell me, you're aunt controls the drug game in all of Memphis. You can't fight that in six months. Even the gangs listen to her. How do you win?"

"Hey, even Tom Lee saved thirty-two people, and he couldn't even swim." Jupiter grinned.

"So, is this about a park being named after you once you're dead? That'll be soon."

"I have the Gangster Disciples ready to roll with me. The other gangs will come along as well. They hate my aunt and uncle. The gangs don't care about anything but the bottom line. My aunt's ship is leaking. I got to make sure it sinks."

Jupiter finished talking and waited on Miguel to finish processing his plan.

"It's stupid, but it can work, I guess. You already have people working for you around the different schools and on the streets. Offer a better price, and they start shopping with you. I think what it comes down to, do they trust you and can you trust them. All it takes is for one person and you're done."

Jupiter contemplated what he just said. It was true all it would take was one person and his plan would be destroyed right along with his future. "They're like slaves. They want a better life too."

"Not all slaves want to be free," Miguel said slitting his eyes at his friend. "This is about trust. If they come along with you, they only become your slaves. Transfer of ownership. You just need to trust them. Can you trust them?"

Jupiter huffed. He knew Miguel was right. "You're right, but I don't have the luxury of not trusting them if I want to do my plan."

"I'm in," Miguel said.

Jupiter was confused about what he was talking about. "What are you taking about? In what?"

"I'm going to help you get out of this. That's what friends are for."

"Hell nawl, I can't do that," Jupiter said totally rejecting the notion. "That's not smart."

"Why not?"

"You don't know anything about this business. It's deadly, and you could end up dead quickly. I can't afford to lose another close friend to this."

"You need somebody you can trust. That's me." Miguel pointed at himself. "I'm not taking no for an answer."

"You know this isn't as glamorous as TV portrays it to be. No one relaxes in this business. Everyone is paranoid and distrusts each other. If it wasn't for Penny, I would have disappeared by now."

"What do you need me to do?"

"I'm still not sure you should be in on this. You're my friend."

Miguel grinned. "I'm not taking no for an answer. So, how can I help?"

"I will need to lease a house for us to stash weapons, drugs, and for us to meet up. And make sure it has a swimming pool. Now that I have my driver's license, I'm going to buy me two identical cars. One car people will know about and the other a secret. Can you find the house?"

Miguel grinned. "I won't let you down."

"Now you're in. Miguel, I'm serious, no turning back now. You're a captain. I don't know what your father does, but if you get caught you're going down like the rest of the crew. Can you handle that?"

Miguel nodded. "So, if your plan works, what happens with your aunt and uncle?"

Jupiter exhaled. "Exactly what they deserve will happen. I want to take you to see something. Also, I'm going to introduce you to Darius. "He's the guy who wants them dead just like me."

❧

After school, Jupiter took Miguel over to the storage locker that Gideon had. The locker was more like a large bedroom. It was set up like a gun show with guns of all types hanging on the walls and on tables around the room. Miguel was in awe. He wanted to back out and tell Jupiter he couldn't be a part of his plan but didn't want to be looked at as being scared. He felt obligated since he had to convince Jupiter to let him in. Jupiter saw the fear in his friend's eyes.

"I won't think any less of you for backing out now. This is a journey that I have to take. You don't. You're always going to be my boy."

Miguel cleared his throat with tears in his eyes. "I'm in this with you."

"Ok, I'm not asking you again," Jupiter said picking up a Glock Nine. "Hopefully, we won't have to use these." He glanced over at Miguel who was ready to throw up.

From behind them came Darius. He stared at Miguel strangely.

"What's up, Jupiter?" Darius asked giving him a pound and a hug.

Jupiter quickly introduced Miguel. "Darius, I want you to meet my best friend. I trust him with my life. He's going to work for me."

Darius laughed. "That's your life not mine. So, did you make the connection?"

"Yep, first shipment is this Friday. I need you to pick it up for me. I can't let Justine or Uncle Tony know I'm behind any of this."

"I got you covered. My guys are ready to jump ship. Her and fuckin' Uncle Tony won't know what hit them. When this is all said and done, I want to be the one to put a bullet in his ass," Darius said with anger.

"Tell us how you really feel," Miguel said.

Everyone was quiet as Darius thought about his comment.

"Little dude got jokes. I might learn to like you, but don't get it twisted with trust." Darius smiled at him. "Do you know who I am?"

Miguel looked into Darius's dangerous eyes. "Yeah, you're the head of the Gangster Disciples."

Darius smiled at him. "No, I'm your new best friend. We are all in this together. I'll get the Vice Lords and the La Raza Nation onboard. We are ready to do this, right?"

"Definitely," Jupiter said. "Come May, I'm out of here. I'll turn everything over to you."

"That's good to hear. I'm going to make sure you get to Harvard or wherever. You might not come back, but I will still brag about you. You're one smart ass kid." He nudged Miguel's arm. "Are you smart like him?"

"He's real smart," Jupiter said speaking for him.

"Not as smart as Jupiter. He's genius level," Miguel replied.

"I better watch out for you two, I see. Einstein created a bomb, what are you two going to create?" Darius laughed. "I got to get out of here. I'll see you on Friday. I'll come by your school, and we can talk about the pickup then."

"Nice meeting you Darius," Miguel said putting his hand out to shake formally.

Darius laughed at his extended hand and gave him a hug. "We family now." Darius strolled off.

CHAPTER FIFTEEN

About fifteen miles away from his aunt's house on Nicolet Drive, Jupiter and Miguel stood outside of a light blue six bedroom home looking at the huge white pillars and the huge red door. It was a surreal moment for them both. Jupiter wanted his plan to work, but had his own reservations on whether some of the things he wanted to achieve would happen. They smiled as the realtor came over from behind them and handed Jupiter the keys. Miguel handed the realtor a briefcase.

"It's all there, the entire hundred and twenty-five thousand," he said smiling hard.

"You boys are quite the businessmen. Just don't get in too much trouble. I'm putting my neck on the line as well."

Jupiter looked at him and smiled. "You're neck has been overly compensated."

The realtor saw the intent in his eyes and backed down. "I'm just saying enjoy. If there are any problems and the police come over, just remember that you are house sitting for your uncle. Call me, and I will take care of it."

Jupiter put his hand out and the realtor shook his hand. "It's going to be great working with you. That money covers the rent and a tip for you for the entire year. If things go as planned, I will double your tip at the end of the year. How does that sound?"

"You're the perfect tenant. I'm getting out of here, boys. Take care and remember to call me if anything happens." The realtor rushed off.

As he was driving away, Jupiter turned to Miguel. "Where did you find that guy from?"

"Hey, you wanted a nice house, and I got it. Sometimes the best people to deal with are the ones who crawl out from under that rock."

Jupiter smiled. "Well, I guess we know where he's headed." They laughed. Jupiter held up the keys. "I owe you big for this one, Miguel."

Miguel fanned him off with his hand. "You don't owe me anything. You made me a captain, and I hadn't done anything. I'm trying to earn my stripes in your crew."

"You deserve it," Jupiter said, walking towards the door. "Let's see what the good life is about." He opened up the front door. The foyer was a wide open space that led directly to the double staircase that met on the second floor. Off to the side, they took a gander into the living room, which was like a grand ballroom. Then they headed up the stairs on opposite sides of each other. At the top they looked back down.

"Look at this place. Who did he say owned this spot again?" Jupiter asked.

"That one football player who played for the Titans and got traded."

"That's crazy. The Titans are in Nashville. That's too far to be heading home after games."

"I'm sure he owned a spot there too. That cat had an eight year, hundred and twenty million dollar contract."

"And got traded after two years. Half of that was guaranteed money."

Miguel shrugged his shoulders. "His loss, your gain."

"You're right about that. We need to furnish this ASAP."

"Really, we talked about this. By next week, this place will be completely furnished and the pool cleaned."

"That's what I want to see," Jupiter said as they raced down the stairs to the backyard to where the pool was located.

When they got back there, they also saw the mini basketball court.

"Man, I wish I could buy this house," Jupiter said with his mind dreaming of the possibilities.

"The plan is not for that. We do this one year, graduate, and get out of Memphis. I'm going to college, and I will be mortified if you didn't."

"Pay no attention to me. I'm just getting wrapped up in the moment. I haven't had shit my whole life. You're used to this life."

"Dawg, you are going to get this and more. Harvard is going to help you network with the real criminals and turn your millions into billions."

They grinned at each other. Jupiter glanced at his watch.

"I better get back before my aunt starts wondering what's up."

"So, what are you going to start telling her about where you're at?" Miguel wondered what kind of lie he was going to tell her.

"That's why I got the two cars. One will be parked at the university library so they think I'm studying and doing college apps. That way I can move around undetected."

"Smart idea buying the two cars. By the way, what did you get on your SAT?"

"I don't know yet. Did you get your scores back already?" Jupiter asked puzzled why he hadn't gotten his.

"I got it yesterday."

"How'd you do?" Jupiter asked.

"Eighteen fifty."

"That's good. I don't know how well I could have done with everything I went through the night before that test."

"I'm sure you did decent."

"Let's get out of here. Next week, I'll have the crew come over and we will lay out the whole plan to them. I discussed it already, and they are on board. I just want them to see what kind of ship they are getting on. So make sure the place looks tight."

❧

When Jupiter got home, Penny ran up and gave him a big hug. It surprised him. When they walked in the family room, everyone was gathered inside and a cake was on the Cadillac modeled pool table. He stared around at everyone, wondering what was going on.

"You're the smartest brother ever," Penny said hugging him again.

"What are you talking about?" he asked, bewildered by her admiration.

Behind him came his clueless cousin Jabari. "Did Pops get a new car?" he asked.

"Be quiet," Justine said.

"What'd I do?" Jabari asked, getting upset that his aunt had shut him down.

Justine went and wrapped her arm around Jupiter' shoulder. "My nephew never ceases to amaze me." She showed him his SAT score paper. "You scored a perfect score. I am so proud of you. Jabari, you need to take note of this."

Jupiter was stunned looking at the paper himself. Remembering the night before the test and the shooting made it seem almost impossible for him to achieve such a feat. Despite the fact that his aunt had opened his mail, he was elated by the news. He hugged her, Penny, and everyone else in the room. This was the greatest piece of news he had received yet. He said a silent prayer, knowing that another part of his plan had come through. As he made his way back around, he noticed his aunt holding something in her hand and was dangling it for him to see. He approached cautiously.

"For you Jupiter," she handed him some car keys.

"What's this for?" he asked apprehensively.

"I got you a Mercedes SUV like mine, yours is blue. I know how much you like that color." She smiled at him and gave him a hug. "You are going to be the first in this family to make something of yourself. I'm proud of you."

Jabari walked off glaring at everybody as he went to the game room down the hallway.

The gift demoralized Jupiter's spirit. It was a grand gesture that now caused a big wrinkle in his plans. He couldn't say no to a three hundred thousand dollar gift from her that everyone would expect him to drive. Seeing him in another vehicle would seem odd, and in some eyes, sneaky.

"Now, I have two cars," he said with a sad chuckle.

"I told Brian he could have your car now," she said. "You've graduated to bigger things. One day, I see you returning the favor to me." She saw a little hesitation in his facial expression. "You don't want Brian to have your car? He's one of our top guys around here now."

He bit his bottom lip. His eyes met Brian's. "No, of course not. Brian's family."

Justine whispered in his ear. "Plus that is an old car. Who drives a Hyundai Genesis anyway? People who can't afford real luxury." She smiled at him.

Uncle Tony came in the house and whispered in Justine's ear. They rushed off. Jupiter wondered what caused them to leave so abruptly. He hoped it wasn't anything about him. Brian made his way over to him.

Brian was a seventeen year old foster kid who had been with Justine for a little over two years. He started as a look out and made it to one of her street captains.

"Hey Brian," Jupiter said trying to read Brian.

"Yo Jay, I didn't want your ride. Your aunt pushed it up on me," Brian replied defensively.

"No need to apologize. Did you talk to her about anything?"

Brian paused for a moment to think about his question then realized what Jupiter was alluding to. "Definitely not that. I'm in. I'm not talking to anyone about that. You might have to worry about Willie. He was running his mouth today on the block talking about a change is going to come. Some of the gang members even down at the pool hall were trying to feel out what he meant. I told him to be quiet."

"Good to know." Jupiter gave him a pound. "Let's get some of this cake."

∽

The following week, outside by the pool at the new house on Nicolet Drive, Jupiter was holding a secret meeting with his captains and some new kids that he felt he could trust from his school. The house was now fully furnished and looked like a house fit for the rich and famous. In all, there were about five people there, Jupiter, Miguel, Brian, Ronnie, and Willie. Jupiter didn't waste any time in explaining to them the risks and the rewards for jumping ship. He told those who worked for Justine, like Brian, Ronnie, and Willie, that they would quit working for her and start selling their product to the dealers and gangs at the lower rate. Jupiter then told them that he would tell Uncle Tony and Justine that they had been spooked by the police and had disappeared. He would supply them with new product. After he finished the statement about supplying them with new product, that's when the questions started.

"That's fine that you will supply us, but is she going to find out who's her competition? No way in hell am I going back on that same block to sell," Ronnie said. "They gonna kill us."

"Ronnie, just listen." Jupiter wanted him to have an open mind.

"I'm not trying to sign my own death warrant on your behalf. I don't see any incentive leaving Justine. Sorry."

Jupiter looked him in the eye. He couldn't believe he was now telling him this. "Nobody's going back to where they were selling. Your selling on the street corner days are over. Our customers are now the dealers on the old corners and the new dealers that we will recruit. I have mapped out locations that haven't been touched and are heavily populated by traffic at night. We got the green light to operate in some old areas and new ones. Nobody will bother us. We also are going to hit the university hard. Students want drugs, and that's what we are going give them but at a better price. You will make more money than you could even dream of."

"Won't we lose money?" Brian asked.

"At first yeah, we will be under-cutting our competition. After a few months, we gradually raise the prices and increase our profits. Plus we will be making money from our new corners. I'm not saying it's going to be easy, but you will reap the full benefits in a few months."

"Okay, I see your plan has possibilities, but why would anybody support a new crew in the city. Your aunt got the police behind her. We got just you. No offense," Brian said. "That's not strong enough."

"This is the freedom we all want," Jupiter said. "That's why I thought you guys wanted in."

"Who said we were slaves?" Brian asked.

"Look around Brian. You're seventeen years a slave," Willie said. Willie was the oldest of them all at twenty-one.

"Jupiter, everyone doesn't have your future," Ronnie said.

"What about the backlash from Justine?" Brian asked. "She's going to come after the person going against her."

"We got guns. She got guns. But if it comes to a war, we will be smart," Jupiter said intensely. "You're right, she will find out, but she won't have the manpower from the streets to fight us. Nobody wants their best deal dead. Who she going to turn to?"

"She still got the gangs," Ronnie said.

"Not all of them. We got protection. The GD's and Vice Lords are going to be onboard once I get you guys in place."

"Damn! That's tight, I'm in," Brian said smiling. He now loved the plan. "You should have said that at the beginning."

Ronnie and Willie still didn't seem as impressed.

"You guys got to trust what Jupiter is saying. It can work," Miguel said drawing a reaction from the others there who had no clue to who he was.

"Who the hell is this guy?" Ronnie asked looking around to see if anyone else knew who Miguel was. "Am I supposed to trust him?"

"He works for me just like everyone else. I trust Miguel just like I trust all of you. We need to be a team. No secrets, no backstabbing, and nobody can let anybody from Justine's crew know what's going on. New corners, you pick your own crew, you can live here for free, but nobody can know you live here, not even your crew. Take them hoes to the Star Motel on Presley Boulevard, not here." Jupiter laughed.

"Why is that?" Ronnie asked.

"People will talk. That's for my safety as well as yours. I'm still living at Justine's and acting like every day is every day. I'll get a new crew on your old blocks. They won't make any money. Justine will start bleeding soon."

"You really going to take out your aunt?" Brian asked.

"If there was another way, I would love to take it." Jupiter shrugged his shoulders. "That's where we have to vow to one another that we won't roll on the organization," Jupiter said. "It's very true there is no I in team. We have to live up to that."

"Are you saying we should die before telling them something?" Willie asked.

Jupiter stared into each one of their eyes. "A coward dies a thousand deaths, a soldier dies but once. Who are you? I want to see a show of hands that's with me."

Unanimously, everyone raised their hands. Although, Willie and Ronnie seemed somewhat reluctant.

CHAPTER SIXTEEN

Over at Texas De Brazil on Peabody Place downtown, Jupiter was on his first date with Angela. It wasn't his choice to take her out, but after her persistence and not taking no for an answer, he figured, why not once. He didn't tell his aunt that they were going out for fear that she would begin to use that against him. He did like Angela a lot and wanted to keep her safe. The night had gone splendidly. Prior to dinner, they had caught a movie, which they both enjoyed. It was also great for him, because Jupiter didn't want to talk about himself. But after they finished eating and waited on dessert, there was dead silence.

"That's a beautiful SUV your aunt got for you. She must love you a lot and be very rich. Does somebody play in the NBA in your family? First, the Grizzlies sing happy birthday to you, now this. You're like the Fresh Prince of Memphis."

Jupiter almost choked laughing. He took a sip of his water. "No, why?"

"That car isn't cheap."

"My grandfather left her a lot of money. She's just sharing. I think she's made some good investments," Jupiter said, hoping that would shut her questioning down.

"To have two cars like that and a house with a pool. She must have invested in Apple." She smiled.

"Something like that."

"I still can't believe you scored a twenty four hundred on your SAT. That's insane. You are so smart. I told my parents you're definitely going to an Ivy League School," Angela said proudly looking into his eyes. "I really like you, Jupiter."

He smiled. "You don't even know me."

"Tell me who you are then?" she asked.

Jupiter wanted badly to open his heart to her and tell her his true feelings. But the one thing that he learned from his mother and aunt was that building emotional ties created weaknesses that people would exploit when they were your enemies. He also didn't think she could ever understand some of the choices he had to make in order to survive.

"I just don't have time to get close to you. We both graduate this year and next year, I'll be forgotten by you."

"I doubt it. You're the guy I want to follow across the world. I see a beautiful light at the end of your tunnel, and I want to be there with you." She reached across the table and grabbed his hand. "I know you think I'm crazy, but I feel something deep for you."

He grinned. Jupiter loved that she had deep feelings for him. "What do you want from me?" he asked.

"The opportunity." She smiled.

"Opportunity for what?"

"To show you that we can be something special way past Memphis. Let's go to school together. You pick the place. We both have the grades. My parents will pay for me no matter where I go, and I'm sure you are getting a scholarship, or your rich aunt will pay for you." She tightened her grip on his hand. "We can make this work."

Her offer was tempting to him, but his sister Penny came to mind. "I have to think about my sister, Penny. She has to be with me no matter what."

"Is your aunt going to let her come to school with you?" Angela was confused on how Jupiter was going to pull that off.

"Probably not, and if that's the case then I'll be going to Memphis for school."

"Really? You don't trust your aunt?"

"No, I don't trust her. She an alright woman but not to take care of Penny," Jupiter said. "Penny's all I got." He looked down at his watch.

"Are you late for something?" Angela joked.

"What if you, me, and Penny were at school together, would that be okay with you?" he asked hoping that she sympathized with his plight.

"Of course. I just want us to be together."

Jupiter smiled. "Maybe there's hope."

"Maybe," she said, blowing a kiss at him.

Jupiter's phone vibrated. He glanced at it.

"I got to take this call," he said, rushing towards the front door. He stopped right outside the front door. "What happened?"

Brian was on the other end. "The GDs, the Lords, and La Raza Nation are with us as long as we can supply them on time. They are giving us a short window to prove ourselves. Are you sure these people are legit?"

"They will deliver as planned. Do you think they are gonna tell Justine or Uncle Tony?"

"Jupiter, they don't care about the politics. They like the profits they will get from the new deal."

"Justine is going to hit the roof."

"Sure will. Some people said Uncle Tony had been asking about us leaving."

Jupiter smiled. "That's good to hear. How are the crews coming?"

"We're getting there."

"We need to be on them blocks by this weekend. In the basement, in the closet, there is a panel behind it that pulls open. All of the product is there."

Jupiter's other line beeped.

"Hold on," he said answering the other line. "Hello."

"Where the hell are you at?" Uncle Tony said yelling through the phone.

"I'm out with a friend. Why you yelling?" he asked.

"Justine wants you home right now. We just got word that the GDs, the Lords, and La Raza Nation are backing out of our deal. We need to figure who the hell is behind all this shit going on. We might have to get ready for war. All hands on deck."

"Why?" Jupiter asked.

"Hey ass, if I knew that answer, I wouldn't be calling you. Get your butt home now!" Uncle Tony hung up the phone.

Jupiter clicked back over. "Brian, it's working. I'll talk to you tomorrow at the house."

Jupiter went back inside and sat down next to Angela and gazed into her eyes. "I know it's a while from now, but how would you like to be my prom date."

She grinned endlessly. "One dream has come true. I think I'm really falling for you."

"I think I'm going to catch you." He leaned in and kissed her.

❧

In the basement office, Justine and Uncle Tony argued about what had happened and how nothing was being done. Their tempers flared up. The more they thought about it, nothing made sense. In the back of each one's mind, they blamed the other.

"People are trying to renegotiate with us, and you don't know why?" Justine asked. "Things happen for a reason."

"You think I'm behind this?"

Justine stood there thinking of an appropriate response. She needed Uncle Tony on her side. In her mind, accusing him wouldn't be smart business. "Of course not. We have to figure this out."

"We can go to war," Uncle Tony said gritting his teeth.

"Tony, it's a war we can't win right now. With the gangs finding a new supplier, they are not going to help us in some street war where they will end up paying us more."

"Let's lower our price to be more competitive," he said.

"Never. I'm not lowering anything. We got to find this supplier and make them see who runs this town."

Jupiter walked in the office. They stopped talking.

"What took you so long?" Uncle Tony asked raising his tone to get his point across.

Jupiter ignored him and looked over at his aunt. "Angela, told me to tell you hi, again."

Justine smiled. "That's a real pretty girl. I'm glad you took her out."

Uncle Tony was disgusted. "What is this, a dating game? Who cares about this girl? He needs to be focused on them streets."

"I am focused on them. Yeah, we lost three dealers, but I replaced them instantly," Jupiter said making Uncle Tony's point moot.

"And you still haven't seen Willie, Brian, or Ronnie?" Uncle Tony asked staring directly at him to read if he was lying or not.

Jupiter slit his eyes at his uncle. "Should I? They aren't important anymore."

"You two need to stop it," Justine said, shaking her head. "I need to figure this out. I think there has to be a connection between us getting hit, your three soldiers disappearing, and the GDs and Lords walking away from our deal. La Raza Nation walking away, I get that. I hated dealing with them fools anyway. The closest crew capable of supplying that much weight is in Little Rock. I can't see them making that kind of move. This is our territory!"

"That's kind of far for them to come unless they got help. That's almost a hundred and fifty miles," Jupiter said.

"You're right. Somebody in Little Rock has flipped. They're working with the Feds." Justine pounded her fist into the desk. "That bastard is trying to kill us all."

"Who is, Auntie?" Jupiter asked, unaware of who she was referring to.

Justine glanced over at Uncle Tony and then back at him. "Nobody for you to be concerned about."

Her comment fired Jupiter up. He didn't like being treated like an outsider. "I thought we were in this together."

"Your friend's father has been tracking us. He has to go," she said.

Jupiter was in shock. He knew there wasn't much he could do once Justine had decided his fate. "What about Miguel?" he asked hoping his friend would be safe.

"If he's at home, and he makes a move then he's gone too. We're not baby sitters. It's a job. Uncle Tony, put Jimmy on this one. I want it done cleanly. No witnesses."

"What about his family?" Jupiter asked.

"I don't have feelings for them. If they are home, Jimmy will take them out."

"His mother and two sisters go to the gym every Monday and Wednesday night." Jupiter wanted to at least save his family if he could.

Justine stared over at Uncle Tony. "Jupiter, you can't get attached to people outside of your family like this. It can lead to your death."

"How will killing his father solve our problem? Our issue is distribution."

Justine laughed. "That fool put his hands on me. I know you didn't think he would see another Christmas. I need you to keep them ears open. Somebody knows who's undercutting us, and they will be bragging to the high heavens that they are getting over on me." She showed them four fingers. "Now, we're the Four Fingers. Somebody is going to show themselves, and when they do, I will move in so quickly and cut their throats and whoever is distributing to them. I'm getting my city back in order. You can best believe that. I'm going to kill that Darius too. He has something to do with this. Getting all sensitive with Clyde dying. Bitch ass."

❧

The very next day in the lunch room at school, Jupiter sat across from Miguel silently. Throughout the hour, he barely said a word and hardly listened. He wanted to warn his friend of his father's pending fate. Jupiter understood that if he did tip off Miguel's father, it would ruin his overall plan of getting his aunt out of the way so that he and Penny could leave Memphis and never look back. The last thing he wanted was to become a witness against his aunt. Knowing her ruthless reputation and how no one had ever lived to testify against her was a thought he carried with him. Seeing the unknowing face of Miguel hurt him deeply. He knew Miguel loved his father and that his father loved him. Their relationship was something he admired. Weighing his options, he forced himself to block out what was soon to happen. He looked up at Miguel.

"How are things going?" Jupiter asked.

Miguel smiled. "Mad crazy. We are making insane money by the campus. We got some real soldiers out on the streets."

"Anything I need to know about?" Jupiter anticipated some bad news following the good.

"Willie was telling me that your uncle has been digging to see who we are," Miguel said cautiously. "But nothing has happened."

"What do you mean by digging?"

"He had some of his people try and rough up the dealers on your old blocks. There was a shootout. Nobody died. Willie thinks he knows where we are getting our stuff from. Have they said anything to you yet?"

"Nothing," Jupiter said wondering where Willie could be hearing all of this news when he hadn't heard anything.

"Are they on to you?" Miguel asked. "Willie knows more than you, and he's in hiding."

Jupiter frowned. "Something doesn't seem right. What else Willie say?"

"He did say something about Uncle Tony planning to kill some FBI agent."

His comment got Jupiter's full attention. "What else did he say about the FBI agent?"

Miguel shrugged his shoulders. "That was about it. I had to go deposit the money in the bank."

"How is that coming?"

"Good. My uncle is taking care of it. He set some offshore accounts for you, me, Willie, Brian, and Ronnie. Darius handles his own accounts."

"He's an honest guy right?"

Miguel was a little taken aback. "That's my uncle. He wouldn't do that to me."

"What about us? He doesn't owe the rest of us anything. Not trying to offend you, but I don't know him. If you say he's cool then I'm down."

"He's cool. Nothing's going to happen to your money, I promise."

"So your uncle won't tell your father?"

"My uncle is the black sheep of the family. He doesn't care where the money come from. He only cares about his five percent cut to clean it for us."

Jupiter smiled. "I can't wait until this is all over with."

"It's going to be hard to walk away from this life. I don't think I will ever make this kind of money so fast in my lifetime. And we don't even have to pay taxes on it. Crime does pay," Miguel said with sparkles in his eyes.

"I'm done on June 1st. I'm going to take my money and go to whatever school that accepts me and disappear from this life. I'm never coming back to Memphis."

"Never?" Miguel was shocked by his response.

"Miguel, there's nothing here for me. Except Penny and I'm taking her with me. And I plan to forget all this drama." The darkness behind his eyes lit up. He felt like the end of his troubles were near. He envisioned his freedom and had a flash thought of him and Penny driving past the leaving Memphis sign.

"So June 1st you're out? What about the summer?"

"I don't know, maybe travel abroad. I have had French for four years now. It would give me a chance to use it there." He smiled.

"You in Paris? I'll believe that when it happens."

"Something good has to happen. This life is killing me fast."

"Just think how much money we could make doing this for just five years," Miguel said foaming at the mouth.

"You think it's fun. This business has a very dark side. You think you're immune to the police or another crew taking you down. No one is. Eventually, all drug dealers get arrested or murdered."

"You've made it."

Jupiter looked at him out the corner of his eye. "I'm just lucky I started at the top. This ain't a movie where the street hustler becomes the kingpin."

"We can beat the odds," Miguel said.

Jupiter thought what Miguel was saying was utter nonsense. "Don't have me regret bringing you in."

Miguel saw the seriousness in Jupiter's eyes. "I'm sorry, but this is like a movie to me."

"Be serious about this life. Nobody stops shooting cause the director yells *cut* in this film." The lunch bell rang. "Hey man, I'll see you tonight at the house. Is your family still going out of town?"

"Hell yeah, my mom and sister are going to Michigan to visit my aunt for a whole week. Just me and my dad and he ain't never home." Miguel winked at him. "I'm gonna have a gang of hoes over."

Jupiter got up from the table, laughed, and walked off.

๛

That night, Jupiter got home and went directly to the bedroom he shared with Penny. He noticed that she had a lot of brand new clothes. It concerned him that she was becoming too close to his aunt. Penny was sleeping.

"Penny," Jupiter said waking her up. "I told you to say no to Auntie about getting all these gifts. You don't need them."

Penny was out of it and tried to focus on her brother's face. "Jupiter, I'm tired."

"I don't want you to keep taking gifts from Auntie. I'm not telling you anymore," he demanded.

"Uncle Tony got them clothes for me. He wanted to see how I looked in them."

Jupiter hit the roof. He snatched Penny out of bed. "What'd he do to you?"

Penny was scared. "Nothing."

"Did he touch you?" Jupiter asked fearing her answer.

"No Jupiter, he didn't touch me. I want to just sleep."

Jupiter thought about saying more. Seeing his sister's tired eyes and almost limp body, he gave up and let her fall back to sleep. He ran down the stairs with some scissors looking for his Uncle Tony. Jupiter searched the first floor of the house and couldn't find him. He walked down to the basement and ran into his aunt. She saw the aggression on his face.

"What's going on Jupiter?" She looked down at the scissors in his hand. "Did Uncle Tony do something?"

"I told him to stay away from Penny. She doesn't need anything from nobody. I got her," he said huffing. "I don't need his sick ass or anybody doing anything for her."

"Penny is my responsibility, not yours!"

Jupiter walked up on his aunt. "You are not Penny's mother," he said raising his voice.

Justine cut him with her eyes. "Better check your tone. I'm not one to fuck with. I'll cut you in half with a snap of my fingers."

They had an intense stare down. While they stood there, Justine reached into her purse on the desk and grabbed her gun. Jupiter got a glimpse of her nickel plated twenty-five caliber gun. He knew she wouldn't hesitate in shooting him so he backed down.

"I'm sorry," he said taking a step back.

She put the gun back in her purse. "I'll talk to Uncle Tony, but you don't run this house. Get your own house and then pull that shit on somebody who cares. Get the fuck out of my face."

"Tell Uncle Tony to stay away from Penny," he said.

"How come you can't find out who's moving in on my corners? Uncle Tony is not your issue. Your issue is them corners. You don't want me to get deeply involved. Heads will roll."

"All I know is that they are some out of town dudes offering a better price. The GDs and the Lords and a couple of the Mexican gangs have been getting their product through this new distributor."

"That's who I want to know. They need to be dead."

Jupiter turned to walk away.

"Jupiter, have you heard from your mother?" Justine asked.

He stopped in his tracks. "No, why?" he asked, curious by her question. Jupiter figured there had to be a rationale behind it. His aunt was a very calculating woman who didn't inquire about fluff.

"Just wondering. I had a dream the other night that she reappeared with Clyde." Jupiter didn't respond. "You remember Clyde came back, and someone killed him. Isn't it odd that Maggie didn't come back with him. He was the love of her life. Loved him more than you two."

Jupiter frowned. "I don't see her ever coming back here. Especially now with Clyde's death."

Justine smiled at him. "I guess you're right. She would have to be crazy to come back here without my money."

"I'm going to bed, Auntie. Good night." Jupiter played it cool. He acted like everything was good. He knew he needed to take out Uncle Tony or soon he would be molesting Penny.

"How's school coming?" she asked before he was able to get out of the room.

"It's going good. I'm just thinking about what college I'm going to next year."

Justine looked down at her watch. "Yeah, we'll have to talk more about that later."

"About what?" Jupiter didn't see a point in a later discussion on his college choices.

"Good night Jupiter," Justine said picking up her phone to make a call. He didn't understand her abrupt ending to their conversation so he stood there. She saw him just standing there. "Good night, Jupiter!"

He turned and walked out of the room. Jupiter figured out that her plan was to keep him in Memphis and in the drug game.

On the other side of town at Miguel's house, his mother was washing dishes as his father sat in his recliner watching ESPN highlights. Miguel's sisters were sound asleep.

"What time is Miguel coming home?" Sylvester, Miguel's father, asked as he looked at his watch. "He's been coming home very late lately. I hope he's not hanging out with that Jupiter Jones kid. That family is trouble."

"He's at the library. Your son wants to go to Harvard. Needs to finish the school year strong, honey. You have to learn to trust him," Miguel's mother said as the dog in the backyard barked and then quickly stopped.

Sylvester put the TV on mute. "What was that?"

His wife shrugged her shoulders. "I'm here washing dishes. Quit being so paranoid."

"I'm not paranoid, just cautious. You need to ..."

Before he could finish his sentence, his wife was shot in the head. Sylvester went to go get his gun, but by the time he turned around, Uncle Tony and three guys had grabbed him.

"You'll never get away with this," Sylvester said bravely. "I'm a federal agent."

"Did you ever understand that we run Memphis?" Uncle Tony asked. "Ten years of tracking us and no results. You're a waste of government funding."

"What do you want?" Sylvester asked as he looked over at his wife's dead body.

"I'm a nice guy," Uncle Tony said looking over at his boys. "I would never break up a relationship." Uncle Tony then shot Sylvester in the head a couple of times.

CHAPTER SEVENTEEN

T he next day, at school, Jupiter saw all the sad faces in the hallway as he was walking towards his locker. Right when the bell rang, his cell phone vibrated. He saw that it was Miguel.

He answered. "Man, you're late for school today?" On the other end, Jupiter heard crying. "You alright?"

Miguel stopped crying for a minute. "Someone killed my parents."

Jupiter was in shock. He couldn't believe Justine and Uncle Tony had killed his mother as well as his father. He thought to himself, "They were supposed to wait until next week."

"Jupiter, you still there?" Miguel asked, wondering why there was complete silence on the phone. "I need your help. Who could have done this?"

He fought every urge to tell Miguel who was responsible. He knew it would only lead to more questions and to how long he knew it would happen. Jupiter felt sorry and selfish for his actions. Hearing Miguel's heart pour out over the phone was earth shattering to his spirit. If ever he felt compelled to help someone it was now, but his guilt stopped him.

"I don't know man. Where are you?" Jupiter asked.

"At my uncle's house."

Jupiter looked at his classmates heading into class. "Text me the address, I'll come over. You shouldn't be alone going through this shit right now. Did anything happen to your sisters?" He prayed the answer was no.

"No, they were sleeping when it happened. When I got in from the other house I found my parents dead. The police even thought I had something to do with it. They said it was a professional hit. The people used silencers."

"I'll be right over," Jupiter said hanging up. The hallway was now empty.

As Jupiter was beginning to leave, a white kid ran up to him.

"Hey, Jupiter have seen Miguel today?" the kid asked.

Jupiter saw that he had been roughed up by someone. "What happened to you?"

The kid was hesitant about telling Jupiter what had happened. "Just tell Miguel I'm looking for him."

Jupiter snatched up the kid by his arms. "What the hell happened?"

The kid was fearful of Jupiter. "The football players down in the gym took everything from me and my crew down there. They said they run the school."

Jupiter fumed. "Where are they now?"

"They're getting ready for gym."

"They said they didn't care what Miguel had to say."

Jupiter reached in his backpack and grabbed a nine millimeter gun out and put it in the smalls of his back. "Let's go."

Jupiter and the kid made it to the locker room area quickly. The boys were still getting dressed.

"Who was it?" Jupiter asked, looking at the kids in the locker room.

The kid pointed at the culprits. "It was Winston and Lamont. I think your cousin is behind it."

Jupiter saw Winston and Lamont. Winston and Lamont looked at him, daring him to do something. Jupiter went over to them and, without a word being spoken, he beat them down to a bloody pulp with his hand gun. The kids around them were in awe of how Jupiter had just annihilated two linebackers from the football team. His cousin, Jabari, ran into the locker room and grabbed him from behind. Jupiter hit him in the mouth with the gun. Jabari fell to the ground. He saw a different, more violent Jupiter, and it scared him to death.

Jupiter ignored the fact that Jabari was even there. He spoke directly to Lamont and Winston. "I want my shit back within the next thirty minutes. If there's some of it missing, or if the money is a dollar short, your life is going to be short. This is my school." He looked at the other kids in the locker room. "If you run your mouth on what you just saw, I got some for you too." He put the gun back in the small of his back, went over and washed his hands. After he finished, he walked out of the locker room as if nothing had just happened. The boys who had just been beaten up scrambled to put their clothes on. Winston and Lamont looked to Jabari for help. He got up dejectedly and walked away himself.

Jupiter got to Miguel's uncle's house. It was a somber scene. He went and sat next to his friend on the couch. When he sat down, Miguel got up.

"Let's get out of here and walk. I need to breathe. I feel like I'm suffocating," Miguel said crying again. "I can't take it here."

"Come on, let's take a drive," Jupiter said giving his friend a side arm hug.

Miguel looked over at his family members huddled in the kitchen. "I'll be back later. I'm taking a ride with Jupiter."

His family was encouraging. They waved him on, knowing that he needed to think about something besides what had happened to his parents.

For the first five minutes in the car, they were both silent. Neither one knew exactly what to say to one another. The loss of someone close and dealing with disappointments were things that Jupiter was very used to, but this was a little different. His guilt felt like a noose around his neck. To him, this was the second time a person had died because of him.

"They are saying that whoever killed my parents was part of a case my father was working on."

"He tracks terrorists, right?" Jupiter asked looking at him out the corner of his eye.

Miguel let out a deep sigh. "My uncle told me he had been tracking down drug dealers in the Southwest. Maybe he got too close." Miguel looked over at Jupiter who was driving. "Do you think your aunt could have done this?"

Jupiter knew in this case the truth would not set him free, so lied. "No, this isn't her style. She probably would have killed you and your sisters too."

"I just don't know what else to do. I can't believe this has happened to me. It's just me and my sisters now."

"Did your neighbors see anything?"

"Not really. Some say they heard the dog give out a strange bark, and some of them said they saw a white older car, like from the sixties or seventies, speed down the street. They even killed my dog. Heartless people."

"You haven't pissed anyone off, have you?" Jupiter asked, thinking about the incident he had before he left the school today.

"No, why?"

"I just had to deal with some shit at school because some of the football players thought they could run you. Don't nobody steal from me."

"What'd you do?" Miguel saw the malevolent intentions in his eyes.

"I did what had to be done. Won't nobody be touching my crew anymore," Jupiter said with a little smile. "The man I worked for had one of the biggest companies in New York City, but he didn't own his own company, the white man did, so they owned him, nobody owns me though." Jupiter laughed to hide the pain as memories of his last conversation with Gideon resurfaced.

"You can't lose your cool man. That could affect you going to college."

"I had to make a statement. They were going to roll over on you. Once that happens, we're done. Nobody respects a punk on the streets."

"So, now, I'm a punk," Miguel said getting upset at Jupiter.

"That's not what I'm saying. We have a reputation to protect, and I made sure they knew who the boss is."

"So much for subtlety."

"Hey man, I'm not here to discuss business," Jupiter said changing the subject. "How are your sisters taking it?"

"Devastated. My mother and them were heading to Michigan next week. It all seems surreal. Jupiter, you can't go undercutting me like that. That's how people will stop respecting me. I would have handled it."

"You're done man. I got to put you on the bench."

Miguel looked at him like he was crazy. "Why you say that?"

"With all that has now happened to you and your family, this is no time masquerading around like a drug kingpin. I got to put you on the bench," Jupiter said, shaking his head.

"You can't do that to me right now. This is all I've got. You guys are my family."

"What about your sisters?" Jupiter asked. "They need you."

"My situation isn't like yours. My sisters will be fine with my aunt and uncle. They have always been nice people."

"The police are going to be sniffing around your house for a minute. You said so yourself that they thought you had something to do with it. We can't afford that kind of heat right now," Jupiter said as he pulled up in front of the house on Nicolet Drive.

Miguel looked at the house. "So what now?"

"Darius wanted me to bring you by. He felt bad when I called him on the way to your aunt and uncle's spot about what happened."

Before Miguel could even respond, his car door opened up, and Darius gave him a bear hug.

"You know you family. If there is anything you want, I got you. I lost my parents when I was young too. My mom died of breast cancer and my father, I never knew that dude."

"Thanks D, it feels good to know somebody cares about you. I'm just at a loss on who could have done this. I want them to pay."

Jupiter tried to get Darius's attention before he responded but was too late.

"Shit, this has Justine and Uncle Tony written all over this. Your dad probably found something out on them and got too close," Darius said. When he finished speaking, he noticed Jupiter staring at him.

Miguel turned around to Jupiter. "Your aunt did this?"

"Like I told you, I don't think this is her style. She doesn't leave witnesses."

"Uncle Tony is a little sloppy," Darius said.

Miguel looked at Jupiter directly in the face. Darius looked at him as well. "Jupiter, did you know they were targeting my father?"

"No," Jupiter said with a straight face. "They typically have everybody paid off."

"My father wasn't the type to take bribes."

"What did you tell the police?" Darius asked Miguel, wanting to make sure he was not a subject of discussion.

"Nothing. I ain't no snitch," Miguel said, understanding the real reason behind the trip to the house. "I told the police that I was at the movies."

"They gonna check on that," Darius said, sounding off the mental alarm.

"I did go to the movie last night. Bought a ticket, went in, lights went off, and I snuck out. Showed them my receipt and everything. I only did stuff like that because my dad would question me to check to see if I was lying."

Darius patted him on the shoulder. "I knew you were smart when I met you. My man."

"Jupiter can you do me one favor." Jupiter nodded, saying yes. "Just find out if your aunt and uncle had something to do with what happened to my parents. That's all."

"I will," Jupiter said. "Come on in, let's hang for a minute. You know I got you."

"We got you little dude, don't worry about a thang," Darius said, wrapping his arm around Miguel.

Jupiter, Miguel, and Darius walked in the house somberly.

⋙

That evening, Jupiter entered the front door in a rage. He put his gun in his front jacket pocket with the intent of using it. The merciless killing of Miguel's mother was an extreme measure that he felt was unjustified. Killing Miguel's father, though he objected, was understandable based on him putting his hands on his aunt. Jupiter wanted to put an end to it all tonight. Without stopping, he went directly to Justine's office to speak with her. What remained on his mind was why the plan had changed from the doing it the following week.

As he got to the office door, Justine saw the anger on his face as he knocked.

"Come in," she said with one eye on him and the other on her twenty-five caliber nickel plated gun on her desk. If it came to it, she was more than willing to use it.

"Why did his mother have to die?" Jupiter asked sadly. "You were supposed to wait until next week. They were going to be gone then. He lost both of his parents."

Justine chuckled. "Sounds like you two have something in common now."

"It's not right! Why are you so evil?"

"What's not right is how you beat up your cousin today at school. His mouth is jacked up. You knocked out one of his teeth."

"That fool came from behind me and tried to grab me."

"He told us that you are running your own little side business at school. Is that true?" She glared at him.

Jupiter shook his head. He didn't want to show the cards in his hand, so he smiled. "Yeah, I'm beating him up and others because of that? You need to ask him what he and them football faggots are doing on my turf." Jupiter asked.

"He is your cousin. Play nice."

"Play nice. You just had my best friend's parents executed."

"What do you expect for me to do? There's a war going on out there. I can't fight everyone at the same time. His father did a cardinal sin when he put his hands on me. I wanted to kill him the night of your birthday. Your friend should be happy that I gave him extra time with his father."

"Is Penny sleeping?" Jupiter asked, realizing he hadn't seen her on his way in the house.

"No, she wanted Uncle Tony to take her to get some ice cream."

Jupiter started to jump across the table on her. "Why did you let him do that?"

"He's harmless."

"What do you think he does with these little girls around here? He's had his eye on Penny. He's sick. You know it!"

"That's my brother."

"And that's my sister."

"You don't want that war, Jupiter," Justine said staring him down into the ground.

"If it involves Penny, I don't have a choice."

"Let it go."

Jupiter stood there thinking about what his next action should be. His heart was squeezed and cutting off his oxygen. He knew he had to play it cool. "Make sure Penny comes to our room when she gets in."

Justine was amazed at how he deflated their intense conversation. "Yeah," she said feeling weird about their interaction. "Also, your school called and said that you were being suspended for fighting."

"You should ask that bitch ass bitch Jabari. I'll take care of it tomorrow." Jupiter left the room without saying another word.

❧

The next morning, Jupiter walked into the principal's office, much to the chagrin of his staff. Jupiter sat down in front of him. The principal jumped up and started to grab him.

"I wouldn't do that," Jupiter said, as he stared at the principal.

"What's wrong with you, young man? You have been suspended for ten days. We have witnesses saying that you beat up two of our football players with a gun. You're lucky I don't call the police right now on you," the principal said walking over toward his desk phone.

"Call them," Jupiter said with an air of cockiness.

The principal picked up his phone receiver.

Jupiter stood up. "I think they would love to know everything you do on the weekend. My boy was Gideon, remember him?"

The principal put the phone receiver back on the hook. He stood there waiting to see what else Jupiter had to say.

"I can bring you down like that." Jupiter snapped his fingers. "But that isn't what you want."

"You don't have any proof," the principal said smugly. "I have witnesses."

Jupiter chuckled. "You think I don't have you on tape? My crew is the one who serves you. That's me on them streets."

"What do you want?" The principal realized that Jupiter was not bluffing.

"This is how this is going to play out. You're going to lift my suspension and say that there is no proof that I was even there. You can tell everybody that I was with my friend Miguel who had just lost his parents the night before."

"People saw you yesterday."

"People saw Jesus yesterday and life goes on," Jupiter said. "I'm not about to allow you to ruin my chances of getting into Harvard, Yale, or Stanford. You better do the right thing, and now."

"What if I don't?" the principal asked.

"If you don't, I'm just suspended, while you're going to prison. I just put a quarter of a key of cocaine in your car. Hard time my friend."

They stared at each other for a few seconds until the principal hit his intercom button. "Jackie, come in here real quick," he said.

Jackie, the administrative assistant, ran in. "Yes sir, what can I do for you?"

"Make sure all of Jupiter Jones's teachers know that he's not suspended. Make sure to remove it from his academic file."

"But there were three witnesses who said they saw what happened," Jackie said eyeballing Jupiter and the principal.

"Who's the principal here, Jackie? Make it happen now."

She rushed out of the office.

Jupiter let out a silent sigh to himself. He couldn't believe his bluff had worked. He had no hard proof of the principal buying drugs outside of the one time he sold some to him.

"Can you please take those drugs out of my vehicle?" the principal asked as he went over and took a seat in his chair. "Is there anything else I can do for you?"

Jupiter walked over to his desk and put both hands down on it. "Yeah, there is. From this day until my last, I run this school. If you think of telling on me or any of my guys, I swear it will be the biggest mistake of your life. I got the goods on several of your teachers."

"What do you mean?" the principal asked, shocked that he wasn't the only one. "Give me names."

"You think you had the market sold up. This higher education mantra doesn't really work here for all your teachers. Maybe the high part does. Anyway, I don't want any more trouble out of you young man. You be good," Jupiter said, smiling as he walked out of the office. He then suddenly came back in the office. "Who snitched?"

"I can't tell you that."

Jupiter smiled with demon eyes. "I think you can."

"Someone left a note under my door. Now please leave my office."

"I'll be back," Jupiter said, winking at the principal as he closed the door behind him.

CHAPTER EIGHTEEN

T he past three months had been wonderful for Jupiter. He had gained the respect from everyone in the entire school, teachers included, in one way or another. Having avoided suspension after beating two student athletes to a pulp gave him legendary status. The fear of him grew immensely, just like the hate for him. His business had thrived, and Justine still hadn't figured out that he was her new competition. She had discovered that the distribution channel was coming out of Little Rock, Arkansas, but hadn't decided what to do about that yet. She didn't want to start a war not knowing who she was really fighting. Through it all, he remained the top student in the school. Though no one knew for sure, word was that the snitch against him in the beat down was his very own cousin, who now hated him more than ever.

Sitting in front of the class taking an exam, Jupiter had his head down and was almost done as a fellow student came to his classroom door. He didn't notice until his teacher came to his desk.

"Are you almost done?" the female teacher asked.

Jupiter didn't look up. "Give me one second." He finished writing and looked up at his teacher. "Yes?"

"They need you in the office," his teacher said, passing the note to him. He looked at the note, but all it said was to send Jupiter Jones to the office.

"Ok," Jupiter said, walking out of the classroom door heading toward the school office.

He saw the back of a woman's head in the office at the counter and thought it looked familiar. He ignored the familiarity of the head and walked on into the office. Inside he noticed the principal and the woman, who he could now see was black. The woman turned around, and he almost had a heart attack. Jupiter could not believe that it was his mother standing in front of him. She ran to him and gave him a hug, which he rejected.

"Don't touch me," he said raising his voice.

"Jupiter, please use my office," the principal said with a fearful expression on his face. "I can take a walk around the school. Take as much time as needed."

Jupiter walked into the office, and his mother followed.

"Why are you even here?" he said, standing next to the principal's desk. "Nobody needs you anymore."

She gazed at her son with admiration. Maggie didn't know what to really say since he had just rebuffed her hug. "You have grown so much," she uttered out softly. "I've missed you and Penny so much."

"Just answer the question, why are you here?" he asked coldly staring at her.

Maggie started crying, which made Jupiter even more angry. He rolled his eyes.

"I messed up. I know I did. I'm sorry."

Jupiter laughed out loud. "You amaze me. You come up to my school and think a sorry will make me forget that you left us at a bank robbery. I really wish you would have just put us up for adoption. You're the worst mother ever."

"I love you," she cried. "I'm much better now. I'm clean."

"You must need something. What is it?"

"Clyde's dead and ..."

He interrupted her. "The man you put in front of your kids. So sad, but I don't care about that shit. You should have died with him."

"I know you hate me, but I need your help. My sister is going to kill me," Maggie said looking around like Justine would walk in the office at any moment.

"Just die," Jupiter said. "I don't need this right now." He got up to leave. She grabbed his arm.

"Please don't go. How's Penny?"

Jupiter turned away from her. "Nobody misses you."

Maggie was on the verge of exploding. Seeing the older and more in control Jupiter talk down to her was devastating and demoralizing. As crazy as it might have been, her expectations had been that she would apologize, and things would return back to the way it used to be before she had left. Jupiter's transformation into the hardened criminal who cared about few things and even fewer people took her by surprise.

"Can I see Penny?" she asked, hoping he would have sympathy for her.

Jupiter laughed. "You think Aunt Justine is going to allow that?"

Maggie rolled her eyes. "I want to see my daughter."

"I want you to leave, but that doesn't seem like that's going to happen for me. Like expecting your mother to be a mother."

Maggie lunged out at him to slap his face. He caught her by the forearm. "You don't have that right anymore." He tossed her arm aside and walked toward the door. "You really shouldn't have come back," he said as he left the office.

Maggie stayed there for a couple of minutes crying her eyes out. As she was leaving, the school bell in between classes had rung. She locked eyes with Jabari and walked out. Jabari quickly grabbed his cell phone and made a call to his father.

"Hey Pops, I just saw Aunt Maggie up here at school."

Uncle Tony didn't know what to say. He was shocked that his sister had actually come back. "Ok," he said as he hung up the phone.

Jabari didn't understand his actions at all. He had thought his father would have been overwhelmingly happy with this news. Hearing the disappointment in his voice made the moment very bittersweet.

∽

Like bees to honey, Uncle Tony ran up on Jupiter when he walked in the house that afternoon after school. Not even letting him put his backpack down, he ordered Jupiter to follow him down to Justine's office in the basement. Jupiter figured that it had to be about his mother by how emotional and erratic Uncle Tony was acting. When he got to the office, Justine seemed rattled. He noticed she wasn't her normal pragmatic self. Her hands trembled as she smoked a cigarette. A habit that she gave up five years ago. Jupiter sat down in front of her. Uncle Tony stood blocking the doorway behind him.

"Hey Auntie," Jupiter said with a smile. "You want to see me?"

Justine glanced at Uncle Tony first then focused her attention back to Jupiter. "Anything happen today that you would like to tell me about?"

Jupiter looked over his shoulder at Uncle Tony. "Is this about Maggie coming to see me at school?"

Justine huffed while Uncle Tony rolled his eyes. "What did she want?" Justine asked.

"Nothing!"

"You expect us to believe that she came back here and risked getting caught to see you and ask for nothing? You better tell more truth in that lie kid," Uncle Tony said puffing out his chest.

"You want to know what we talked about?" Jupiter rolled his eyes at Uncle Tony.

"Don't be rolling your eyes at me," Uncle Tony replied back.

"Jupiter, I just want to know why she came back. Is she somehow behind my people jumping to a new distributor?"

Jupiter sighed. "No. Maggie was there acting like she cared about me and Penny. She wanted to see Penny, and I told her we didn't need her. I told her to leave me alone and not to come back. You think I would want anything to do with her? Hell no. She's the reason for all my problems."

Justine saw his point but was still thinking there was more to tell. "She didn't say anything else about why she came back now."

"If she was going to say more, I didn't give her a chance. The sight of her sickens me."

"Where's she staying?" Uncle Tony asked.

"Why don't you ask the person who you got spying on me?" Jupiter asked standing up defiantly. He looked at Justine. "Is that all? I got homework to do." She nodded her head, and he walked out of the office.

"You believe that shit?" Uncle Tony asked his sister.

"Yeah, I do. But that doesn't mean we don't keep an eye on him. She will contact him again. Maggie wants to see Penny and won't stop until she does. I know my sister."

❧

It had been a memorable Valentine's Day for Jupiter. He had just come back from a date with Angela. They had gone to dinner and a movie. He floated inside the door thinking about their kiss as he dropped her off at home. He had resisted getting close to her due to her safety being jeopardized, but his heart and love for her succumbed to her great love for him. When he got in his room and undressed, he paid little attention to his sister curled up in the bed silently crying. He laid back on the bed and smiled at the ceiling as he heard a whimper coming from Penny's bed. He went and checked on her.

"Penny, why are you crying?" he asked, looking in her face.

She didn't say a word or look at him.

"What's wrong?" He pried. Jupiter could tell something had happened. Penny tightened her eyes to avoid seeing his face. "Penny, you better tell me right now what happened?"

Penny opened her eyes and a gush of tears ran down her face. "He touched me."

"Where?" Jupiter demanded.

His voice struck fear in his sister. She saw the danger in his eyes and knew he wouldn't stop hounding her for answers. "Down there." She cried some more.

Jupiter left her side and put his clothes back on. He reached under his bed and grabbed a gun he had taped under it. He went back to Penny, kissed her on the forehead, and told her to go back to sleep. Jupiter then rushed down the stairs and went directly to Uncle Tony's room. His gun was drawn as he entered. It disappointed him that no one was there. Back in the dark hallway, he stood wondering what his next move should be. With it being late and everyone asleep, he started thinking exactly where Uncle Tony might be so that he could kill him tonight. A bright idea of where Uncle Tony might be hit him, Jupiter quietly walked out of the house unnoticed. Instead of driving his car, he walked down the street until he saw a neighbor's bike on the lawn. He grabbed it and rode off.

It took him about an hour of hard riding, but he finally caught up with Uncle Tony at a hole in the wall breakfast restaurant near downtown. He noticed that Uncle Tony was all alone and had just started eating. He wanted to rush in the restaurant but waited across the dark street in the alley, staring and waiting for his moment to approach his uncle without any witnesses.

About halfway through the breakfast, Jupiter saw Willie go inside and sit down with Uncle Tony. He began gasping for air wondering what Willie was going to tell, or had told, Uncle Tony already. It was killing him inside knowing that his grand plan, which was just four months away from its June completion, was probably now destroyed. He watched intently trying to read their lips and mannerisms to see what they were discussing. After Willie and Uncle Tony finished breakfast, they got up and hugged each other and walked outside.

Once outside, they went their separate ways. Jupiter watched as Willie drove off and Uncle Tony walked to his car. Instead of Uncle Tony leaving, he sat in his car smoking a cigar. Jupiter looked around to see if anyone was in the area and if there were any surveillance cameras near Uncle Tony that would catch him on camera. Once he saw the coast was clear, he ran over to Uncle Tony's car and shot him point blank in the chest two times. Uncle Tony tried to grab his own gun but was too hurt to grab it. He stared at Jupiter as he slowly died.

"You think you're going to get away with this sneaky shit," Uncle Tony said coughing up blood. "You're a dead man!"

"You too, you sick fuck," Jupiter said as he shot him one more time, but this one was in the head. "Bye bitch."

As he raced back into the darkness, he couldn't help but think about how he needed to deal with Willie and alter his plan moving forward. By the time he reached home, Jupiter knew he couldn't risk dying so easily by being within Justine's four walls. He went inside with the plan of packing up both his and Penny's clothes and moving to the house he was renting out. With such a short time left before his graduation and departure from Memphis, he just wanted to be free. When he got to his room and saw that Penny was not in her bed, it sickened him. He knew she was in the room with Justine. He tiptoed over to Justine's room and quietly opened the door. His stomach turned even more seeing Penny in the bed next to her. For a few moments, he contemplated getting Penny out of the bed, but on second thought he figured Penny would start a big fuss and resist going with him so he just as quietly closed the door. Returning to his room, he packed up his things and jumped in the SUV his aunt had bought him and left. As he drove away, he couldn't believe he had left Penny.

In a parking garage downtown, he parked the SUV. He walked outside and got in the car with Darius.

"You sure you don't want to go get Penny?" Darius asked.

Jupiter glanced down at his watch. Sadness overcame his face. "It's too late now. I have to figure something else out."

"Don't worry about your safety. I'll make sure you have people around the clock watching your back. Justine loves Uncle Tony like you do Penny."

"We got to get Willie," Jupiter said, trying to not think solely about leaving Penny behind. "I can't believe he sold us out."

CHAPTER NINETEEN

T he next morning, the police came to Justine's door looking for her. Looking out the window at the police officers, she called out to Uncle Tony, but got no answer. He was the usual person to answer the door.

"What the hell do the police want with me at this time in the morning?" she asked herself slowly opening up the door.

In front of her stood two black police officers. Their faces were sad, and you could tell they were a little intimidated by her stature in the city.

"Ma'am, I'm sorry to disturb you, but do you know an Anthony Lamont Jones?" the officer standing directly in front of her said.

"That's my brother. Did something happen to Tony?" she asked as her heart pounded and her face became flush.

"Yes, about three a.m. this morning, Anthony Jones was found shot dead in his car."

Justine laughed it off like it was some type of joke. "Who put you up to this?" she asked looking past the officers.

After a moment of silence, she stared at the officers and saw that this was no laughing matter. She cried, but didn't break down screaming like a woman who had lost her best friend. Justine kept it together the best she could.

"Where is his body?" she asked. "And who shot him? How was he shot, from the back?"

"No, the person shot him at close range right in front of him. His body is in the county medical examiner's office, and we have no idea who shot him. That's why we need to talk to you."

"Why don't you ever have a clue? This is my only brother. I want somebody to pay for this," she said as if ordering them to do it.

"Ma'am, we don't have any witnesses. He was eating at the diner, and the waitress and owner said he came there regularly," the officer said. "Do you have any idea who would want your brother dead?"

"I'm not doing your fuckin' job for you. Find who killed my brother and then maybe we can talk." Justine closed the door in their faces. When she turned around, Penny was staring up at her.

"What's wrong, Auntie?" she asked in her little voice. She saw the stream of tears on Justine's face.

Justine was quiet until she thought about the officer's question of 'who would want your brother dead'. "Where's Jupiter?" she asked Penny.

"I don't know," Penny said, not understanding what was going on. "Why were the police here?"

"I want to see your brother now!" Justine yelled in anger. Penny was terrified. She had never seen or heard her aunt yell like that. Justine saw the terrified look on Penny's face. She felt bad. "I'm so sorry, Penny. Auntie doesn't mean to scare you. Something happened to your Uncle Tony, and I need to ask Jupiter about it. Have you seen him?"

"Yeah, he was here last night."

"Did something happen between him and Uncle Tony?" Justine asked trying to put the pieces together.

Penny didn't want to say. She could tell her aunt's intentions of finding Jupiter were not good. Justine saw the hesitation in Penny's eyes.

"What is it Penny? Something happened, didn't it?" Justine was losing her patience. "You better start talking."

Penny turned away from facing her. "He touched me last night." She began crying.

Justine used her hand to turn Penny's face to look at her. "Who touched you and where?"

"Uncle Tony. He touched me down there. He wanted me to get undressed. I cried, and he told me to go to my room and to not say anything to anybody," Penny said slowly.

"And you told Jupiter this, didn't you?"

"I told him last night when he got home."

Justine shook her head in disgust. "Are you sure Uncle Tony touched you? Or did your brother tell you to say that?"

"I'm not lying, Auntie, I swear." Penny stared into her eyes.

Justine could tell Penny wasn't lying. It tore her apart knowing that her brother was dead. She had known about his sick habits for years, but never thought he would prey on Penny. That was the line she had told him to never cross. For this indiscretion, she wanted him dead, but not at the hands of her nephew, Jupiter. In her weird way, she still wanted the person responsible to pay, even though it was Jupiter.

Justine then rushed up the stairs and into Jupiter and Penny's room. She went through his closet and dresser drawers and found them empty. She sat on the bed and started crying as Penny came and joined her.

"Did Jupiter run away?" Penny asked with deep sadness. "Is this my fault?"

Justine wrapped her arm around her. "This is not your fault." She sighed. "Where would your brother go? Did he say anything to you?"

Penny shrugged her tiny shoulders. "I don't know. I wish he would come back."

Justine slit her eyes. "I'm not sure he's ever coming back here."

Penny burst into tears. "I thought he loved me."

"He does love you, but sometimes people never come back. You always have me."

"First, my mother and now Jupiter. I'm all alone."

Justine tightened her arm around Penny. "I'll never leave."

"It's not the same." Penny pulled away and curled up on the bed.

Justine stood up and went and looked out the window. "Have you heard from your mother, Penny?"

"No," she said mumbling from her pillow.

"I need to talk to Jupiter. If you speak with him, you need to tell him immediately that he needs to call me." Justine despondently walked out of the room, wondering what else Jupiter might be up to.

Across town, Jupiter was standing by his bedroom window looking down at the cars and the people passing by. He had barricaded himself in the room. In his hand was a Colt Forty-Five pistol. On the bed was a semi-automatic machine gun and two sawed off shotguns. He anticipated that Willie had, by now, told Justine everything about their plan and about the house where he was living on the side. He kept looking at the clock on the wall, expecting an army of Justine's street soldiers to come after him. As the minutes became an hour, he didn't know what to think then he saw a familiar face walking up to the door. He smiled and quickly unblocked the door. By the time he finished, Miguel was standing at his bedroom door. They hugged.

"What's going on, Jupiter?" Miguel asked, glancing around the room and seeing the guns on the bed.

Jupiter put the gun he had in his hand in the smalls of his back. "Nothing, why you ask?" Jupiter tried to play coy.

"I'm your best friend. I know that much about you. Something isn't right."

"I don't want this to be your concern," Jupiter said going over and sitting on the couch near his bed. "How are you doing?" he asked, trying to turn the tables.

"I was doing fine until I came in here and my boy looking like Malcolm X. Just tell me what's going on?"

Jupiter didn't want to tell his friend about how he had killed his uncle or why. The thoughts of killing him wasn't the painful part at all; it was the fact that he had left Penny. Seeing that Miguel wasn't going to stop questioning him, he gave in.

"My uncle's dead."

"Good," Miguel said. "I'm glad somebody finally got him. Who did it?"

Jupiter looked at him. Miguel didn't know how to respond. Assuming that Uncle Tony had killed his parents, that made him happy, but knowing that Jupiter could kill him in cold blood scared him.

"He touched Penny, and I knew it would only get worse. I had to stop him."

Miguel nodded then asked, "How do you feel?"

"I don't know." Jupiter felt weird discussing it. "What are you up to?"

Miguel saw a lot of Jupiter's clothes on the bed. "Is your aunt coming after you?"

He slit his eyes at Miguel. "I don't know. I wasn't going to stick around and find out. That was her brother."

"What do you know? Is Penny here with you?"

That struck a chord with him. Jupiter rammed his fist in the wall. "I had to leave her."

"What happened?" Miguel was in disbelief that he actually left the sole reason for his whole game plan.

"I wanted to bring her, but she was in my aunt's bed sleeping. I didn't know what else to do. My aunt won't hurt her that I know. She treats Penny like her own daughter."

"Has your mother come back to visit you? Did she ever see Penny?"

Jupiter hadn't really thought about it, but it did seem odd that he hadn't heard from his mother anymore.

"No to both questions. It's like she just disappeared, which isn't her style. Unless she's dead, she'll resurface."

Jupiter's cell phone starting ringing. He saw that it was Penny and quickly answered.

"Penny, are you okay?" Jupiter asked, happy that she had called.

"Jupiter, Auntie wants you to come back home. Uncle Tony is dead."

"Are you alone, Penny?" Jupiter asked, thinking that his aunt was near Penny. Penny went silent. "You can put her on the phone, Penny."

Justine had been listening to their call. She took the phone from Penny. "Jupiter, we need to sit down and talk," Justine said trying to hold her composure. With her hand, she instructed Penny to leave the room. Penny quickly left.

"You think I'm stupid. You know and I know you want revenge for your sick ass brother's death. He was a menace to society and needed to be stopped. How could you turn your head on what he was doing to those little girls?"

"You're only seventeen years old. How long do you think you can last out there on the streets? If you want to see Penny again, you need to come here to my house. And I will have people around her school making sure you don't see her. You can't run from me."

"I'm not running."

"If you don't come see me, you will be looking over your shoulders for the rest of your life. That's not living."

"If Penny can come with me after we meet then okay. I will come right now."

"You know that's not going to happen in this lifetime. Penny is my daughter now."

Jupiter hung up the phone.

"Hello, hello," Justine said, realizing that he had just hung up on her. "That ungrateful bastard."

Jupiter laughed and put his phone in his pocket. "Another roadblock."

Miguel saw that he thought it was humorous and added to the mood. "I guess you can cancel the prom."

Jupiter almost turned pale. "Shit, I promised Angela I would take her."

"Some promises are made to be broken."

"Not this one."

"Jupiter, how do you plan to go to the prom and not be seen by your aunt? Hell, what about school?"

"School is not a problem. Got enough people to look out for me. Plus, Darius got some guys protecting me. I got to find Willie."

"What's up with him?" Miguel asked. "Darius said he hadn't seen him in a couple of weeks. Not even answering his phone."

"Willie was at a meeting with Uncle Tony last night. He turned on us."

"What are we going to do?"

"You back?" Jupiter asked Miguel. He hadn't planned on ever letting Miguel back in, but now he needed him more than ever.

"Life is boring unless you're gambling with it." He smiled. "Let's play poker, bitch!"

They both laughed.

CHAPTER TWENTY

The following week, Justine had orchestrated the biggest funeral Memphis had ever seen. It was like Uncle Tony was a world renowned political figure or entertainer. With nearly a thousand people in attendance, many of the people were in the hallways and standing outside. In attendance were many luminaries around the state of Tennessee and within the city. Even the mayor and the chief of police were sitting in the first couple of pews. Justine wanted to show everyone the love she held for her dear brother.

As the service ended, a black woman dressed in black with a velvet veil covering her head and face slowly made her way up to Uncle Tony's casket. No one paid the woman any attention as she spit on the closed casket and joined the family as they walked out of the church. By the time they got to the front of the church nearing the exit, the woman had grabbed Penny and ran downstairs and out the back door. When the procession reached outside and the family was ready to get into the limousine, Justine realized that Penny was gone. She scrambled back inside the church and had people looking in the basement to find her. No one could locate her whereabouts. Justine couldn't believe Jupiter was that smooth to grab Penny without her knowing. She had people on look out for him to show up. Not suspecting anyone else to be that brave to defy her, she convicted Jupiter even before having concrete evidence. As she was getting into the limo, she grabbed Leroy, her head bodyguard, by the shirt collar.

"Leroy, you better find her today," she said demanding. "If she's hurt one bit, somebody's going to die over this. I can't handle all this today."

"I'll find out everything possible today, Justine," Leroy said.

Justine slit her eyes at him. "Get my baby back," she said as she got in the back of the limousine.

It didn't take long, by the time the limousine was about to take off, Justine's security guards had brought the velvet veiled black woman and Penny over to her car. Her security guard took off the veil and revealed Maggie. Up until now, Penny had no clue who the woman was behind the disguise. Penny saw her mother and hugged her. Justine wanted to take Maggie right then and there and kill her, but seeing how affectionate and loving Penny was towards her, she couldn't bring herself to ruin that reunion right now. After they hugged, Maggie stopped and stared at her sister.

"She's mine, not yours," Maggie said. She turned to one of the security guards who were holding her arm. "Get your hands off me. Justine, you don't want to cause a scene out here."

Justine looked around. With the mayor, the police chief, and other dignitaries there, she didn't want her family business spread out into the streets. She decided to not act on hurting Maggie at this moment.

"Penny, get in the car," Justine said, opening up the door.

"Can Momma come with us?" Penny asked.

Justine looked into Maggie's eyes. "No, your mommy has some other plans, like visiting Jupiter."

Penny turned to her mother. "Where's Jupiter?"

"I don't know baby." Maggie said. "You go with your aunt. We'll all be together again."

Justine gave her a smile. "Very optimistic," she said as the limousine rode off. About a block down the street, Willie was waiting at the corner. Justine's limousine stopped, and he got in.

"I've been trying to reach you," he said.

"About what?" Justine asked with attitude.

"Jupiter."

"I'm listening," she said as the limo took off again.

❦

Prom night, the most magical night of the year for high schoolers, had finally come. It was hard to fathom how he had survived the last few months avoiding being caught in a trap set by his aunt, but Jupiter somehow did. With the help of Darius, he was protected at all times. At school, nobody came near him. Even his cousin, Jabari, couldn't get close to him, though he did threaten him often. Working with the principal, Jupiter made sure that every kid went through the metal detector. Having friends still at Justine's house, he was able to still communicate with Penny. Though Justine hadn't done anything to avenge Uncle Tony's death or acknowledge that he was her competition, and that made everything seem weird. Willie had disappeared into thin air and everything seemed somewhat normal, except for him not being able to see Penny. Their operation had grown exponentially and the day before, Jupiter had received two acceptance letters, one from Harvard and the other from Stanford. Both were offering him full scholarships.

When he pulled up in the Mercedes stretch limousine in front of Angela's house, he was on cloud nine grinning from ear to ear. There was a car of people in front of and behind him with Darius's people watching his back. He hadn't a care in the world as he went inside her house and chatted with her parents, who adored him. He was the guy every mother and father wanted dating their daughter, he was smart, intelligent, respectful, and had a bright future ahead of him. Though he and Angela hadn't made love, he knew she was without a doubt the woman of his future. And as she graciously waltzed down the stairs and into the living room, he fell in love all over again. Seeing her wear her form fitting prom dress around her hour glass body and looking into her sexy light brown eyes made him weak at the knees.

"You look beautiful," he said upon seeing her.

"Thanks Jupiter."

"Are you ready to go?" he asked grabbing her hand nervously.

"You kids have a wonderful night," Angela's father said, opening up the front door.

They took one last picture then walked off to the limo.

At the prom, it was a perfect dream. Jupiter and Angela danced all night long. It was as if nobody else was even there. Towards the end of the night, not a surprise to many people, Angela and Jupiter were announced as the King and Queen of the prom. As the prom came to a close, Darren, one of Jupiter's classmates, came over to him.

"Hey Jupiter, you don't mind if we catch a ride with you in your limo?" Darren asked.

Jupiter looked out at the marina. "Where you trying to go?"

"Our limo broke down or something. I've been calling this fool for over an hour. Jimmy and I are just trying to get to the Hilton downtown."

"Just take it and tell the driver to come back for me afterwards. I'll text him right now that you guys are coming outside."

Darren smiled. "You're the coolest guy at the school. Thanks man."

Darren took off and went and grabbed his group of friends. They hurried outside to the limo like horny teenagers trying to get to the hotel for prom sex.

Jupiter laughed at his friends and played it off like he wasn't thinking the same. Angela looked at him with a devilish smile.

"You wish you were with them?" she asked.

"Yeah, if you were with me."

"I want to make love to you, Jupiter," she said, making his jaw drop to the floor.

He thought about what she had just said. It was very tempting, he remembered that he had left the three pack of condoms on his dresser.

"We have a lifetime," he said.

"But I want it to start tonight." Angela leaned over and gently kissed him on the cheek and then on the lips.

"Want to go back to my place?" he asked.

"Won't your aunt and all the other people living there be in the way?"

He wanted to tell her about the house that he had been renting and other details of his life, like his aunt is probably trying to kill him, but he stayed silent on that front.

"Yeah, you're right. We can catch a cab to the Hilton," he said. "If you're game, I'm all in."

"Let's do it," she said getting him up. "Call the cab."

On the cab ride over toward the Hilton, they got stuck in a traffic jam. It took over an hour until they got to see what had caused the halt of traffic moving. Jupiter saw it first and tried to shield Angela from seeing the limousine that they were in on the side of the road shot up about a hundred times. When she saw it, she stared at him for a few minutes trying to comprehend what had happened and why. Jupiter, on the other hand, grabbed his phone and called Miguel.

"Miguel, move everything into the panic room and stay in there until I come," Jupiter said.

Miguel was an emotional wreck himself. "It's too late man. They already came and shot up the house. I'm in the panic room now. Willie killed Darius. I'm scared."

"Are the police there?"

"No. They used silencers. I only got away because I had a feeling and started moving things in the room then. I'm the only one who made it," he said.

"Don't leave that room. I'll be there in a minute. Stay put," Jupiter said as he hung up the phone. He bent over and gripped his head. He fought off crying and did his best to not show Angela exactly how much danger they were in.

"What's going on, Jupiter?" she asked with her eyes fixated on the limousine. "They are probably all dead. That could have been us."

Jupiter didn't know how to respond. He wanted to dispute what she had said, but didn't want to lie. He reached over and hugged her.

Angela didn't want his comfort, she wanted answers. "Why?" She started crying as the coroner examined the bodies lying on the ground on the other side of the car.

Jupiter felt compelled to give her answers. Telling her the truth seemed so wrong in his eyes. Involving her in his dirty deeds wasn't what he had planned.

"I don't know. My aunt is into some things that I don't know much about. I just think we are blessed to be alive."

"Who were you talking to?" she asked.

"Miguel, why?"

"Why would you tell him to move everything into a safe room? Something doesn't seem right. Are you in trouble? How is Miguel involved in this?"

"Don't overreact."

"Just tell me!" she said in a high pitched voice.

"I..." Jupiter started to talk then she interrupted him.

Angela's eyes grew big as she interrupted. "It's true what they say about you at school. I didn't want to believe it. Jupiter, you killed them." She pointed out the window at the limousine.

"Angela, this isn't what you think. I didn't know my aunt was this dangerous." He teared up.

"Please take me home," she said pouting. "I want to live a long life. I'm sorry."

Jupiter didn't want to take her home but respected her choice. "Ok, whatever you want."

She nodded. "You're a drug dealer, Jupiter. I believed people were lying about you because of your background. I can't do this. Take me home now."

He handed the cab driver a fifty dollar bill. "Take her wherever she wants. I'm getting out here. Angela, I'm sorry for disappointing you. I never meant to hurt you." Jupiter jumped out of the car and walked across the street. He and Angela stared at each other as her cab drove off. They both couldn't fathom how a night so beautiful could turn ugly so fast. Their hearts broke together that night.

It didn't take long, but Jupiter made it to his neighborhood near Nicolet Street. He cased the neighborhood, trying to see if Justine's people were somewhere near. He slowly made his way to the house. Noticing that the coast was clear, Jupiter went inside. Walking over the dead bodies, he walked over to the panic room. Miguel opened up the door. He walked in, and they closed the door. They sat down on the couch next to each other.

Jupiter could tell by Miguel's face that he had just finished crying. "This is the worst day of my life," he said to Miguel leaning back on the couch. "I was so close, but still far away."

"We need to strike back," Miguel said turning to face him.

"We need to just run. It's over."

"We can't run forever. What about Darius and the others? They joined you because they believed in you. I think we need to fight back."

Jupiter was hesitant. "We're done. We can't win. Miguel, you have your entire life to look forward too. This life isn't your life."

"It is now. My father and mother are dead. I'm an orphan."

"This is all crazy. Graduation is next month. My aunt only wants me. You need to go to your aunt and uncle's house."

"What was it all for?" Miguel asked.

"I'm not sure. I lost everything I tried to keep. I'm tired. I just want to be a kid again." Jupiter bowed his head perplexed about what to do next. He knew Miguel wanted to fight back, but his heart was gone. He lost so much that all he wanted to do was crawl under a rock.

"So what are you going to do?"

"I'm going to head to college early," Jupiter said.

"So you're just going to leave Penny with your aunt, who's a cold blooded killer?"

Jupiter hated the Penny question. Penny was the purpose of it all. Losing her hurt deeply. He grabbed Miguel by the shirt collar with both hands. "What do expect from me? I'm just a seventeen year old kid from the streets. We can't win Miguel. Get it through your head. It's over."

Miguel cleared his throat. Seeing the rage in Jupiter almost made him piss his pants. "Jupiter, you're the smartest kid I know. I respect you. You will never live with yourself if you leave Penny back here. Plus, do you think your aunt is going to stop coming after you? This was a massive calculated hit. She's going to wipe all of us out. You know too much."

Miguel's words hit home. Jupiter knew Justine would never stop her pursuit to erase him from the earth. His fear was losing more than he had already lost. He pondered his options as he released his hold on Miguel.

"I don't even know where to start," he said.

"She has to have some weaknesses."

"Penny and my mother," Jupiter said, shaking his head.

"Why your mother?" Miguel asked.

"I don't know, but she refuses to kill her for some reason. That might have changed now."

"You should find her. It's worth the risk."

"I don't want to, but you're right I need to contact her."

"What do you think we should do?"

Jupiter looked at Miguel. "Finish this shit once and for all." He gave Miguel a fist pound. "I'm going to college and putting this city behind me forever."

"What happened with Angela?"

"I don't want to talk about it," Jupiter said, regretting the night he had with her. The terrible ending erased all of the good beginnings for his prom night.

"Well, no matter what the plan, I want Willie. He killed Darius for no reason and couldn't even face him. I wanted to help, but I was scared. He shot Darius in the back."

"Miguel, there's nothing you could have done. They would have just killed you too."

"That's why I want him for myself."

Jupiter stared into his friends sorrowful eyes. "If that's what you want."

CHAPTER TWENTY-ONE

O ver the past month, Jupiter had hid out in Miguel's aunt and uncle's basement. Scared for his life and trying to plan an escape from Memphis consumed him daily. He still had a lot of money, but the Little Rock, Arkansas connection and street soldiers had been destroyed by his aunt. The house that they had occupied was no longer theirs. All the cars that he had were put in storage and the money was all in the trunk of Miguel's car. It was near the two million dollar mark. Luckily, the realtor who rented the house to them helped him and Miguel out by saying that the people killed in the home were squatters. He did it to save himself as well. Being involved with drug dealers wouldn't have been ideal for his client relationships.

With Justine having re-confirmed her hold on the drug trade in Memphis, Jupiter had little to nowhere to run. His only chance was to graduate and disappear forever. Since the prom, he had been expecting his aunt to come finish the job. Surprisingly, she never came looking for him. None of that mattered to Jupiter, he just wanted to get out Memphis still breathing. Since he already finished his classes, he was able to avoid having to go to school, but he did hear that his cousin, Jabari, was looking for him and threatening his life again. He had thought that he would never see nor need his mother for anything, but in order for him to live a life without constantly looking over his shoulders, he needed help. He connected with her through Darius's old girlfriend. He didn't have a clear idea of the plan he needed to get out of Memphis alive and with Penny, but hoped that his mother would provide some insight to help him beat his aunt.

Jupiter hadn't left the house but once, and that was today, two days before his graduation. In the wee hours of the morning, Jupiter met with his mother near Interstate 40 by Bass Pro Drive. He picked his mother up at the corner and drove off quickly. Jupiter was in Miguel's car, which was a black Ford Mustang with dark tinted windows. Maggie was so grateful that her son had come around to see her again. She was still hurting from the pain that she had caused him and Penny. She had no clue to what he wanted, but Maggie didn't care, this was her chance to be a mother to her son.

Jupiter stopped at an old hole in the wall breakfast restaurant. They got out, walked in, and barely even looked at one another. They sat down across from each other. When the waitress came, they ordered breakfast. Once the waitress left, Maggie looked at her son.

"How are you doing, Jupiter?" her eyes were filled with pain and regret. Deep down, Maggie felt responsible for everything that had happened to him.

Jupiter burst out into tears. At that moment, he was a seventeen year old kid who needed his mother more than ever. "I don't know."

Maggie grabbed his hand and cried with him. "This is all my fault. I know my sorry means nothing. I should've been your mother your whole life. I do love you and your sister."

Jupiter started to bring up the past, but quickly stopped. The past meant nothing to him, and the future was all he cared about. "That's in the past. We can't change that. We've all made mistakes."

"Don't you put any of this on yourself. If I had just been there for you two, this would've never happened. I'm here for you now. If Justine thinks that she's going to kill my son, she's going to have to go through me."

Jupiter stared at her. Her words of defending him made him feel good inside. "How do I make it out of Memphis and take Penny with me?"

"Justine and Jabari both need to die," Maggie said, expressing to him that there was no other way for him to leave without worrying about them in the future.

"Why Jabari?" Jupiter asked. He completely understood the need to kill Justine. Jabari seemed more wannabe to him and not a true threat.

"You killed his father. You're out of the way now, so who do you think is going to step into Uncle Tony's shoes? And if Justine is gone, he's taking over."

"What about college? I know he was planning on going."

She tightened her grip on his hands. "This life is a rush like no other. Jabari has always wanted to be like his father. He will try to avenge his death eventually. You will never have peace."

"I met my father," Jupiter said, taking the conversation off track.

Maggie was stunned. That was a secret she thought no one knew or could find out. "How did you know who he was?"

"Shouldn't write down everything. You left your book the day you and Clyde robbed that bank and left."

Maggie sighed. "I always wondered what happened to it. I thought it was in the police evidence room collecting dust. When did you go to California?"

"Awhile back with Penny. I thought maybe he would take us in and be a father, but Marcellus already had a family he wanted. This asshole acted like he wasn't my father."

"I'm sorry that happened. He was a very self-centered guy when I knew him. He was great at times, but it was all my fault. I should have made him be a father to you."

"You can't make anybody do anything. He should have wanted to be a father. I'm a damn good kid. Why is it that my mother and father didn't want to raise me?"

"Jupiter, we are just idiots. I can't explain what really happened, but I know I made the biggest mistake of my life with you. You have done a beautiful job raising yourself. And you're going to live a long life and achieve great things. That's my promise to you. I owe you so much. Whatever you need just ask."

"I need for you to kill Justine," Jupiter said. He knew no one else could get close to his aunt like his mother.

Maggie responded quickly. "If that's what you need then I'll do it."

"I need it done this weekend during my graduation ceremony."

"Why then," Maggie asked confused.

"Justine will be vulnerable during that time. She will probably have some people at the graduation waiting to grab me after my speech."

"You're doing a speech?" Maggie asked proudly.

"Yeah, I'm the valedictorian for my class. I've worked too hard not to be there for that moment."

"I'm proud of you. Despite my failings, you've made something great out of nothing. Are you going to college?"

"Harvard in the fall. Full scholarship." He mustered up a smile.

"So how am I to get close to my sister and get Penny out of there too?"

By Jupiter's face, it was apparent that Maggie's mission would be deadly. "You have to get caught."

"That doesn't help us. Justine will kill me on the spot. I can't do this unless you guarantee Penny's safety. I can live with dying, but not with her dying too."

"She won't kill you immediately. Justine wants to taunt you with the fact that she's raising your child. I have these two trackers that will locate you wherever she hides you." He showed her what they looked like. "One will be on your shoe lace and the other in a pair of underwear. Her people won't check those areas at all."

Maggie was intrigued, but still didn't see the safety net of getting Penny out safe and alive. "What about Penny?"

"I have a crew of about ten GD's still mad about Darius's death. They will come in right after Justine gets a call from the ceremony that Jabari is hurt."

"What's going to happen with him?"

"I got that end of things covered. I just want you to focus on your part."

"They come in and then what? You still have to make sure that Justine and Penny are in the same location."

"That's the only real guarantee I can give you." With his eyes, Jupiter cut his mother. He wanted her to know that she might not live at all, and that his plan could ultimately fail. "But I do know this is the best play."

Maggie contemplated what he had just said. This meant being there for her kids and, on a small level, her redemption, she was okay with risking her life for them. "I'm in."

Jupiter pulled a cell phone out of his jacket pocket. "Tomorrow, I will contact you on this phone. Make sure you answer it."

Their waitress started to bring their food back to the table.

"Hopefully, you'll come to Harvard to visit. That would be nice."

"Where will Penny be?"

"With me, I'm going to buy a townhouse near the campus."

"God willing I'll be there to visit this fall, but we both know the devil has been watching my back." They both shared a small laugh as they started to eat.

⤜

Graduation day came. The proud parents of the children who would walk the stage were smiling and chatting with other families. As the students lined up, Jupiter was nowhere to be found. From afar, he looked on to see who was looking for him. He did see Jabari combing the line to find out if Jupiter was there. His eyes also caught some unusual people walking around the crowd o. As his eyes wandered, he saw an unexpected person in the crowd, his aunt, Justine. He almost panicked. Jupiter glanced all around her and didn't see Penny. A text message came to his phone. It was a message from an unknown person. The message read, Plan B at 3:30. Jupiter was puzzled by the message. He figured that it was from his mother, but 'what was Plan B at 3:30' was the mystery to him. His classmates walked into graduation and took their assigned seats. Jupiter made his way to the stage, going through the back entrance. When he appeared on stage and took his seat, Justine and Jabari were stunned. Justine had assumed that he had left town forever, but came just to confirm it. Seeing their faces gave him a silent confidence that whatever Plan B was could still work.

At Justine's house, it was just a normal Saturday for the kids. They were watching TV and playing games until they went to the streets to work. Maggie had intended to turn herself over to her sister, but when she arrived and saw Penny playing checkers with another little girl, she decided to just take her herself. She was able to get Penny and walk out of the house unnoticed. Maggie put Penny in her car, and they drove off.

While the principal was talking and doing introductions, Jupiter sat there focusing on whether he would make it out of there alive. In the group of his classmates was Angela, who caught his eye, and they smiled at each other until the principal called Jupiter's name to come to the podium to speak to his classmates. He slowly got up and walked to the microphone. He glanced out at the people in the attendance. At the back by one of the exit doors, he saw his mother holding hands with Penny. Inside he rejoiced and began to speak.

"When I was thinking about my Valedictorian speech and what I have gone through in my life to get here today, I reflected back on Dr. Martin Luther King's 'I Have A Dream' speech. I know I'm only 17 years old, but I feel like I've already experienced 70 years in my young life. Just thinking about the struggle of black people and poor people alike, I know the pains of not having something to eat or heat to keep me warm. Not being able to take that class field trip or buy a new pair of shoes is a real bummer. I know we all praise Dr. King and the dream speech, but I want to know 'When Will Reality Come'?

"Yeah, the world has seen a black President, but how does that translate to me getting fed? I stand on the shoulders of men like Douglass, Garvey, Washington, X, King, and Obama. They have opened doors for many people of all colors, not just black. My people have economically grown at the rate of a turtle, but this is no cartoon. The rabbit keeps winning in my reality. I challenge my people to wake up from that dream and look in the mirror and ask themselves, 'When Will Reality Come'?" He paused and looked out at the crowd.

"The Emancipation Proclamation was in 1865, The Civil Rights Amendment in 1964, but my people still struggle to provide for their families. No matter how you cut it, we're still poor. Poverty plus poverty doesn't equal prosperity. Is the plan to wait another 99 years for real change? Since his speech and his death, we have still been crippled by the manacles of segregation, the chains of discrimination, and fooled by integration. We as black people, we as colored people, are still exiled and despised in our own homeland. Never given credit for our contributions to the America that we helped build into what it is today. It hurts me deeply knowing that my future is in peril because of my skin color, my speech, or where I come from. Should I aspire to be an athlete or rapper? Where are the role models that are not associated with sports and entertainment? If I sell drugs, does that make me a bad guy if I'm trying to survive and support my family? The government does it daily, and nobody tries to arrest them. Is the darker my skin color equivalent to how dangerous I am? Remove the color of my skin, and I am just like you. To be exact, I am you. I'm just the side of you that America cares less about."

Jupiter took a pause and stared at his mother and Penny in the back. Justine tried to see who he was looking at, but couldn't see past the crowd behind her. He also looked in

...gela's eyes, and she looked in his. Angela smiled at him. He exhaled and went back to finishing his speech.

"Dr. King said that he went to the nation's capital to cash a check and that America defaulted on that promissory note, but 'When Will Reality Come' that America reimburses us for the past, current, and future work on building this great nation. How is it fair that a company that has 5,000 white employees and 200 minorities be considered fair and just? Why are there more liquor stores than parks? Why are there more prisons than help centers? Why do the police patrol my neighborhood and not yours? Isn't it funny how police officers always seem to know black kids, but not the white ones? I just want to live in a world where fair and just is spoken from a true tongue and not just words sprung from a mouth to give people lip service. 'When Will Reality Come' to make what's on my mind outdated and a lie. I'm not saying that discrimination will ever end, but I just want my America to realize that many of the people within its sacred borders are in quicksand while the people of privilege walk proudly down that yellow brick road toward that sign that states "For Whites Only and a special few".

"I'm awake! I'm done dreaming! I'm just trying not to drown. My eyes are open now. It's time for everyone to wake up and let reality ring from Maine to Mississippi, from Florida to Hawaii, and from California to D.C. We need reality to show us our fallacies of who we are, so that we can become who we were meant to be. We were put on this earth to be great and to make a difference. You need to become that person. I know I'm trying to. Whether I live a long life or die today, I know that dreaming will get you nowhere. My reality has arrived. Join me in reality. Thank you." Jupiter proudly smiled as he made it back to his chair.

The student body and all the parents stood up, clapping for Jupiter. Even Justine clapped and cried. Jupiter glanced back over to the exit door where he had seen his mother and sister. They were now gone. Now standing, Justine realized that he was looking at the exit door at the back. She figured that his mother had been there. She made a call to her security to look for her sister and to make sure that Jupiter wouldn't get away.

As the principal ended the commencement ceremony and the graduates tossed their caps in the air, Jupiter disappeared in the sea of caps and gowns. Jabari and his aunt looked all over the place and couldn't find him at all. Jupiter had run as far as he could before he ran out of breath. He flagged down a cab driver so he could go to Miguel's aunt and uncle's house, first to grab his duffle bag, and then take him to the airport. When he got to airport and began going through security, he got a text message again from the unknown number, who he was now sure was his mother. The message read, "I am going to be that mother to one of my children. I will see you this fall. Love you." Attached to the message was a picture of Penny smiling.

Jupiter smiled as he walked through security. He had purchased a ticket to Paris to spend his summer before going off to school. When he got close to his departure gate, there was a crowd of people surrounding the bar nearby. Everyone was glued to the TV set. From outside the bar, he saw that there had been a car bomb explosion at his graduation. He felt bad for how things had transpired, but once he saw the plane boarding, he ran to his gate to enter.

∾

That fall at Harvard, after checking in and buying all of his books, Jupiter walked across campus joyously. He couldn't believe that he had finally made it. In the middle of the campus, he crossed paths with Angela.

"Hey Jupiter," she said grinning. "You made it."

"Of course I made it. How are you Angela?" He smiled at her. She was still the love of his young life and by his eyes, anyone could tell he wished that it could be forever.

"Doing great now that I see you're here. What did you do this past summer?"

"I spent it in Paris." he said.

"With who?" she asked. Angela said with a hint of jealousy. "That's a city for lovers."

"By myself, I always wanted to go, and after graduation, I jumped on that plane and took off. It was one of the greatest experiences for me."

"Where's your sister, Penny?"

Jupiter smiled. "Living with my mother in Boston."

"That's close. Your mother is okay now?" she asked, curious about his mother since he hadn't told her any good things about her in the past.

"This move out here is a fresh start for us all. She's been doing fine. Penny is happy that she has her mother again."

"What about you?"

"I'm grown now. Our relationship is different. It's a story in progress."

"I was sorry to hear about your aunt and cousin," she said feeling sorry for his loss.

"I'm so excited to be at Harvard," he said changing the subject. "It's like a dream come true. Memphis is in my past."

She smiled. "Your reality. I never got a chance to tell you, but I loved your speech. My father thinks you're going to be the next President of the United States."

"This is my fresh deck of cards. Let's see how this hand plays out."

Angela laughed then gave him a hug. "Maybe we can grab coffee or something?"

Jupiter smiled as his cell phone rang. "Or something. I'll see you around." He walked off and answered his phone. "What's up Miguel? How's Yale?"

"Better than Memphis."

"At least we're living," Jupiter said smiling.

"Better than your aunt, cousin, and Willie. Plan B was pretty good."

"Memphis is behind us now. Bigger and better fish to fry," Jupiter said. "Man, I forgot about Willie."

"Nothing to remember now." Miguel smiled. "Like a speck of dirt washed down a drain heading to nowhere."

Jupiter grinned. "It's in the past now. Our future is bright. Sky's the limit."

"New location, new people, but the same product. You gotta love America, Jupiter."

"Miguel, that's in the past." Jupiter shook his head.

"You know how many crooks come out of Yale and Harvard?"

"I don't know," Jupiter replied. "You ran the numbers?"

"I don't know either, but I'm sure a lot." They laughed. "I'm trying to be on the top of the food chain, not the bottom."

"I know you're not saying what I think you're saying?" Jupiter asked.

"You're born, you take shit. You get out in the world, you take more shit. You climb a little higher, you take less shit. Till one day you're up in the rarefied atmosphere, and you've forgotten what shit even looks like. Welcome to the layer cake son."

"You and I are probably the only ones who remember that movie," Jupiter said smiling.

Miguel laughed. "Probably so, but that line is true shit. Isn't that part of that reality shit you were kicking at the graduation?"

"Is that speech going to haunt me for the rest of my life?"

"I'm just saying, I met a guy who knows a guy, and we had a little conversation about some things. Some very lucrative things."

"So you're Walter White now?"

"Never that. You'll always be Heisenberg."

Jupiter glanced at a welcome to Harvard sign. "We got enough money. Don't be greedy. We got everything we need."

"Greed is good. We don't have a G7. I don't know about you, but I live under the C.R.E.A.M code."

"What's that?"

Miguel chuckled. "Cash rules everything around me, get the money dollar dollar bill y'all."

"Money isn't everything," Jupiter said with conviction.

"Then why go to Harvard?"

Jupiter thought for a moment about the question. "Man, I just want to make an honest living where I don't have to look over my shoulder every minute wondering if today I'm going to get stabbed in the neck or not."

"Okay, all I'm asking is for you to just think about it. America doesn't give a shit about you or me. Politicians, Corporate CEOs, and billionaires are all out for self. We didn't land on Plymouth Rock, Plymouth Rock landed on us."

"Damn, now you breaking out Malcolm X on me. Do know how much money I got right now?"

"A couple of million."

Jupiter laughed. "Add five to the front and add two zeros. I'll never want again."

"Damn! You got to be joking with me," Miguel said shocked by the revelation. "So, where is the money at? You need to get that G7. So, what are you going to do?"

"I got a plan."

"What is it?" Miguel asked. "I want in."

Jupiter grinned. "Holla at me later," he said as he hung up the phone. "A G7 would be nice." Jupiter glanced up in the air looking at the clouds. "It's time for me to take over the world. That's my reality," he said as he continued his walk through campus.

CPSIA information can be obtained
at www.ICGtesting.com
Printed in the USA
LVOW13s0959190317

527716LV00008B/642/P